SEMINAR IN EVIL

SEMINAR IN EVIL

Daoma Winston

Chivers Press • Thorndike Press
Bath, Avon, England   Thorndike, Maine USA

This Large Print edition is published by Chivers Press, England, and by Thorndike Press, USA.

Published in 1995 in the U.K. by arrangement with Severn House Publishers, Limited.

Published in 1995 in the U.S. by arrangement with with Jay Garon Brooke Associates, Inc.

U.K. Hardcover ISBN 0–7451–2791–6 (Chivers Large Print)
U.K. Softcover ISBN 0–7451–2799–1 (Camden Large Print)
U.S. Softcover ISBN 0–7862–0470–2 (General Series Edition)

The text of this Large Print edition is unabridged.
Other aspects of the book may vary from the original edition.

Set in 16 pt. New Times Roman.

Printed in Great Britain on acid-free paper.

British Library Cataloguing in Publication Data available

Library of Congress Cataloging-in-Publication Data

Winston, Daoma, 1922–
  Seminar in evil / Daoma Winston.
    p. cm
  ISBN 0–7862–0470–2 (large print : lsc)
  1. Large type books. I. Title.
PS3545.I7612S46 1995
813′.54—dc20

For Murray

CHAPTER ONE

The dry dead leaves of November whispered under my moccasins as I turned unwillingly into Dandy Lane, leaving behind me the wide house-lined boulevard that led back to the busy campus. There the tall white buildings glowed with light, and the continuous parade of students, coming and going, made elaborate patterns along the concrete roadways and under the tall spruces.

Here all was empty silence, weighted with somber autumn, the path very nearly an enclosed tunnel through great walls of skeleton bushes. As an antidote to the burden of dreariness, I tried to think of spring, of birds signaling to each other, of golden blossoms aglow in the sun, and warmth on my chilled face, but there was no escape. My usually fertile imagination failed me.

Dandy Lane was gray and ugly and still. I took slow plodding steps through the whispering leaves, and clutched my books to my chest. I rounded the last curve. In the past month I had learned every inch of the way. I knew each loop and turn and had catalogued each shadow, but I had never grown accustomed to any of it. I had never learned to take for granted the strange mixture of repulsion that thrust me back and the yearning

1

attraction that drew me on. I didn't understand how two such conflicting emotions could war within me at the same time.

The last curve was finally behind me. I saw the gross ugly outlines of the house. It squatted like a giant gray toad athwart the blocked lane. Great piles of leaves were stacked around the two tall granite pillars that were the remains of a huge wall that once enclosed the acre of earth and bare trees. The wall was gone now; nothing of it remained except those two pillars, standing like the relics of ancient Stonehenge fallen into decay. Between the two posts a gravel road wound in a circle up to the house, past its steep wooden steps and then back to the lane again.

I paused to look up at the house. A cloud, misty pale and unmoving, seemed to hang over it, muting its faded gray paint. Across the front there was a wide porch, decorated with carved trim that was slowly weathering away. The three floors rose up above it, clifflike and forbidding, to a roof that slanted into pointed gables. The long rows of uncurtained windows watched me, blank and empty as the eyes of the mindless dead.

I drew a deep breath, clutched my books closer, and started up the gravel road, remembering the first time I had come here. I went back over it in my mind, trying once again, as I had so many times before, to understand why I had moved out of my dorm, given up the joys and discomforts of living with a hundred girls, to live instead with the small group from the seminar. There were eight of us, all students in the experimental class in psychology called The Group Mind, Psych. 155. Dr. Henry Paulen taught the seminar. He owned the house at the end of Dandy Lane. Once again I tried to recall who it was that first suggested we all move in together, and once again it was impossible. I remembered only that I had been the last of the eight to accept the suggestion; for weeks I had been the only holdout. I had even written to my parents about it. Was I hoping that they would tell me I must stay in the dorm? I don't know. Perhaps if they had, everything would have been different. Instead they told me to do what I liked. It wasn't what I liked particularly, but somehow I had given in, and, struggling with mixed feelings, I had checked myself off the dorm list, apologized to my annoyed roommate, Helen Byers, and made my home with the others in Dr. Paulen's house.

Now, at the foot of the porch steps, I stopped once more. A faint wind whispered through the leaves and swayed the limbs of the huge oaks that arched over the house. I listened hard for sounds from within, for voices, for laughter, for the hard drum of music. There was nothing. Day after day, returning from my classes, I was faced with the surprising silence. The house seemed to swallow all sound, to will

3

an everlasting hush.

I took a deep breath and climbed the steps slowly. Was it intuition that so weighted my feet? Did I have some foreknowledge of what was to happen? I don't know. I suppose, now, that I'll never know. I remember only that I always entered the house on Dandy Lane with a strange unwillingness, the same strange unwillingness that I felt that early evening, with twilight ebbing into darkness, when I first had a glimpse of the terror that was finally to engulf me, to engulf all of us.

The lower foyer was empty, dark. I called out a muted 'Anybody home?' and the house seemed to sigh around me. Beyond that there was no answer.

I wondered where the others were. They should have gathered here by now. I had dawdled as long as I dared, hoping not to have to be in the house alone. I put my books on the long narrow sideboard. It was made of dark wood, ornately carved and scrolled, but, like everything else in the house, old, unpolished, uncared for.

A small red box was used for mail. I reached into it, hoping that something had been delivered for me after I left for my first class that morning. I shuffled through the envelopes. There might be a quick note for me in my mother's round sloping hand or a few scrawled lines from my father, but I found nothing. I couldn't really understand the wave of longing

4

that swept over me then. I felt, momentarily, as if I were being borne away on swift currents to sink forever beneath them. I had done well in high school, and now, at eighteen, I was a sophomore. I had been away from home, except for vacations, for over a year now. Even before that I had taken trips and had gone to camp every summer. Eighteen was too old for homesickness, but as I dropped the envelopes into the red box, I felt tears sting my eyes. If only ... The rest of that thought glimmered and disappeared.

I blinked away my tears, and peered into the shadowy mirror over the table. Big dark eyes stared back at me, eyes much too large for the narrow white face into which they had been set under thick straight brows. I frowned and those brows drew down. I blinked and sooty lashes rose and fell. I swept my long dark hair off my neck and turned away from the mirror. Staring at my ridiculously woebegone reflection would give me no relief.

It was almost dark in the foyer by then. The upper hall, the top of the wide steep staircase, seemed shrouded in shadows. My moccasins whispered in the thick rug as I went to the light switch and, reaching for it, put a foot on the first step of the stairway.

At that moment, a scream ripped the fabric of silence. It was loud, raw, and achingly filled with anguish. The terrible tearing quality of it froze me. It came again and then again, a great

5

quivering sound that seemed to echo first through the house and then through my heart.

Distorted with horror, it was still recognizable as human. And I knew the voice, the throat from which it sprang, the body out of which it welled. I knew it was Selena Sellers.

The frozen moment, an instant of time that seemed like an hour to me, broke suddenly. It melted away and I was freed. I wanted to turn, to escape into the dark silence of Dandy Lane. I imagined myself dashing to safety far away. But I hurled myself up the steps. I tripped, and lost a moccasin and didn't turn back for it. I pounded up and into the shadows and then down the long hall to the room that Selena and I shared since I moved in a month before.

Even then, breathless, my skin prickling, my heart thudding against my ribs, I knew that the nameless thing I had feared for so long was upon me. I knew that in some terrible way my odd reluctance, my uneasiness, and need to remain aloof, had found their cause. I touched the closed door to the room and it sprang open soundlessly.

Selena lay on the braided oval rug between the desk and the bed. I could see her clearly in the last glimmer of light from the big bare window. Her long blonde hair streamed wildly over her navy turtleneck sweater. Her violet eyes were wide and staring. Her pink mouth was distorted with the continuing screams that shook her slender body and filled the room.

'Selena!' I cried. 'Selena! It's me! It's Jennifer. What's the matter, Selena? What is it?' I dropped down beside her. I caught one of her flailing hands, felt her ice-cold flesh, and a shudder ran through me. 'Selena. Stop it! What's the matter?'

She trembled convulsively. She twisted and writhed and fought the empty air while the screams poured from her straining throat. I grabbed her in my arms and held her tight. I kept saying, 'Selena, tell me. Tell me what's wrong?' hoping I could get through to her.

Slowly, so terribly slowly, the awful sounds subsided into choking sobs. She finally leaned against me, trembling and weeping. My questions became wordless soothing mumbles, offers of consolation and protection. But from what I didn't know.

At last she said, 'So awful! Oh, dear God! Jennifer, it was so awful! It hurt. You can't imagine how it hurt.'

'But what? What hurt?' I asked.

Already I was beginning to review the possibilities. Was Selena sick? Had she been stricken by a sudden terrible headache? Could those things have provoked her terrible screams, those sounds of anguish and of terror?

Her small face was very pale. She turned her violet eyes away from me so that I couldn't read them. She whispered, 'It was the scratching. Tearing me to pieces. I never

7

thought I'd survive it. I never thought I could. It went on and on and on. I don't—'

I cut in quickly, 'What scratching? Who? What?'

'The scratching,' she repeated, but she wouldn't look at me.

'You're not making sense.' I took my arms from around her, sat back on my heels, off balance on one moccasin, and wondering where I had lost it.

'It came while I was working.' She turned her head, looked at the desk under the window. A tremor shook her body. 'I was sitting there trying to read, and suddenly I felt it.' Her voice ended in a choked sob.

I couldn't answer her. I was without words, without questions. I was staring at her throat. Three long jagged bloody scratches marked her white skin. I studied them closely. Then, without comment, I studied her arms. The sleeves of her sweater were pulled up, and both of her wrists were clawed with long angry welts beaded with drops of blood. I didn't know how Selena had gotten them, but the scratches were obviously real.

I got to my feet and went down the hall to the bathroom. I wet a towel with cold water and hurried back to Selena. She was still sitting as I had left her, staring at the desk, but now her face was composed. She let me help her up and to a chair. She accepted the towel and patted her throat and arms. She looked at the

8

bloodstains on it without surprise, but I saw shivers move along her legs, and I saw terror in her violet eyes.

She was a year older than I, but there was something poetic, even dreamy, about her that often made her seem younger. We shared in common an imaginative approach, but she was easily influenced and vulnerable while I tended to be stubborn as a rock.

'It's crazy,' she said. 'Just crazy, Jennifer.'

'Suppose you tell me what actually happened,' I suggested, relieved that she seemed to have gained control of herself so quickly.

'I came back the usual time. I was supposed to meet Jimbill, but he didn't show up, and I decided not to wait. I've got an awful lot of work piling up all of a sudden.' She swallowed. 'Well, anyway, that's neither here nor there, is it? I came up and settled down at the desk. I made up my mind to get something done before dinner, so I was at the desk, with my back to the door. And then—then *it* came in. I was trying to read. I didn't see anything or hear anything. I was just reading, I tell you. But suddenly I felt something reach around and tear at me!' She gasped for breath, struggling to contain herself. 'I know what it sounds like, Jennifer. I can't help that. It's true! It's true! I felt something, somebody, reach around and tear at my throat. I fell back in the chair and held my arms in front of my face. I felt claws

9

tear at my wrists. I screamed and screamed. And then I was on the rug. I could feel it rough against my back, and something was trying to tear me to pieces!' She kept her face turned away from my searching eyes.

I said quietly, 'Selena, nobody was here. You know that. You said so yourself. You just told me that you didn't see anyone and didn't hear anyone, so ...'

I knew my words were useless, but I could find no other ones. She couldn't accept reason, and reason was all that I had to offer her. She didn't answer me. She silently pointed to the scratches on her throat and her wrists.

'I see them, Selena. But still ...'

'All right,' she whispered. 'I can imagine just what you think, Jennifer. I didn't do them myself. That's what you suppose, of course. But you're wrong, I tell you, you're wrong. Something terrible is happening. You've got to believe me. You've got to help me. I swear to you, I swear, I didn't do it to myself.'

Her violet eyes stared pleadingly into mine. Her pale face begged me for belief. But I didn't know what to think. Selena claimed that something unseen, unheard, had attacked her. How could that be? And yet ...

She offered her slender hands to me. 'Look,' she said. 'Look at how short my fingernails are. I've been biting them down again, the way I used to when I was a kid. Just look at them. Could I have torn my skin with my nails this

10

way?'

I glanced at her very short, bitten nails. I turned her hands over and studied her stubby fingers. There was no sign of blood on them, no shreds of skin.

'You see?' she asked shakily, but with a note of triumph. 'You see, Jennifer? Do you believe me now?'

'I know you got scratched,' I told her. 'But how, why? Selena—' I stopped, trying to think of some tactful way to put what was in my mind. I found none so I went on, 'Look, Selena, are you sure you haven't made up this weird story because—Maybe you had a fight with Jimbill?'

She shook her head, and the blonde hair whipped wildly across her face and then fell in tangles to her shoulders.

'Did you have a bad dream?'

'I was reading!'

'But you could have fallen asleep.'

'I didn't!'

'Then could someone, a stranger, have been hiding in the house when you came in? Could he have attacked you while you were dozing, so you didn't realize? And then he ran out.'

She glanced sideways toward the big window. It opened out to nothingness, out to a sheer drop to the hard ground below. There was nothing to climb, nothing to stand on. She didn't have to tell me what she was thinking. No one could have gone out that way.

11

She said, 'You were at the foot of the stairs, weren't you?'

I nodded. That was where I had been when I first heard her scream. I had reached for the light switch, one foot on the first step. I had frozen at the sound of her voice, remaining there for a moment, before pelting up the stairs and down the hall into the room. No one had come down. No one had passed me. I was sure that the other rooms on the floor were empty. Had they not been the others would have gone running to Selena, too. But then I realized that someone might have left Selena, slipped into one of the other rooms and hidden there, waiting until I had rushed past before slipping away. If that was what was done, it was too late for me to go and look. While I had struggled with Selena, the intruder would have made good his escape.

Selena leaned back in the chair and closed her eyes. She twisted her hands in her lap. She said, 'Jennifer, I know you won't believe me. You won't dare. It's too frightening to think about, to try to understand, to face—but nobody was here. Just me. Just me, and...'

I waited patiently, but she didn't go on. Her pale face was still, her eyes closed.

I said gently, 'Selena, finish it. Tell me what you're thinking but are too afraid to say.'

She opened her eyes and looked at me. She took a deep breath and leaned forward. 'It's the Group Mind,' she whispered. 'Don't you

12

see? Don't you understand? Don't you realize what's happened, what we've done? It's the Group Mind, Jennifer.' Her pinched white face was suddenly wet with tears. Her violet eyes gleamed. Her whole body trembled.

The Group Mind? I found myself shivering, too. It was the subject of the seminar we were taking together. Selena, Jimbill, the others that live on Dandy Lane, and me. All eight of us had been studying mob psychology for the past two months, and we had begun a series of experiments to see if we could, within our own small group, create a mind that superseded all of us.

Now Selena was saying that we had achieved our goal, and that what we had made was something that had attacked her. I couldn't believe her. I told myself that it was not possible that we could have done any such thing, but I didn't want to argue with her. I wanted to calm her, and I wanted time to think what to do, how to help her.

I had no time. As I sat there, considering, she suddenly screamed, 'Jennifer, it's back!'

She flung herself out of the chair, stumbled, still screaming, across the room, and crouched in a corner. 'Oh, no!' she cried. 'Oh, no, no! Don't! Don't!' Screaming, she writhed, struggled, and fought against emptiness.

I was on my feet but unable to move. I just stared at her as if held in invisible bonds. I felt a great weight pressing me back, restraining me.

13

I felt a hot heavy burden bearing down on me. It was if I knew that I must not touch her.

She screamed once more, a hoarse, raw, keening note, and then was still. Her body went limp and she sprawled unconscious.

I was suddenly free then. I moved slowly, painfully, as if in a trance, to her side. The three scratches were on her throat. The torn places were on her wrists. She had screamed and cried out, but there were no new marks on her. She said it had returned to the room and attacked her again. She claimed it was the embodiment of the Group Mind. But I had seen nothing, heard nothing.

She opened her eyes as I bent over her, took her hand. 'You see, Jennifer. I told you. Now will you believe—'

The voice from the open doorway was cool, amused, and somewhat chiding. 'What's going on here?' it demanded.

As always, since the first time I had heard it, it touched me in some strange way. It had a timbre that seemed to vibrate in me. Selena, too, had once confessed that it gave her shivers up and down her back. We had laughingly agreed that Dr. Paulen probably affected all the girls that way, whether or not they admitted it.

'Well, what is it?' he went on, standing on the threshold. 'We can't have unaired problems in our family, can we?'

I looked up at him. 'I'm afraid Selena's not

14

feeling well.'

He came into the room, tall, lean, with the careless grace of an athlete. His deepset black eyes moved carefully, consideringly, between Selena and me. A small smile appeared within the black beard that concealed his chin and upper lip. 'What seems to be the trouble?'

Selena gave me a pleading look and, shuddering, shook her head.

I said, 'I don't know, Dr. Paulen.'

His smile tightened. His dark gleaming eyes narrowed. He shook his dark head slowly from side to side. 'We had agreed, I thought, that here, within the family, I would be Hank, and not Dr. Paulen.'

I muttered, 'I'm sorry.'

He raised dark brows in a questioning arch.

'I'm sorry, Hank,' I said.

'Of course. It's quite all right. I'm just sorry that you find it so difficult.' He shrugged, went on, 'Allow yourself to be one of us, Jennifer. That's all that I mean.'

The reproof brought a sudden tightness to my throat. I wanted to apologize. I had to. I yearned to convince him that I was one of the group, truly, but he gave me no time.

He said, 'You do know what happened, Jennifer. Don't you think that you'd better tell me?'

The strange timbre of his voice was almost hypnotic.

I found myself unable to hold back. I

15

gathered strength, preparing to explain, but Selena murmured a quick, 'No, no, it's nothing really. It's nothing. I feel too silly. Jennifer, please don't.'

He bent down, put a lean brown finger on her throat, and I saw her tremble at his touch. 'This is nothing?' he demanded. When neither of us answered, he went on, 'Oh, I don't agree. How can I? Hadn't we better discuss this? After all, we live together. We share our lives, don't we? That was the agreement. Anyone's problem would be a problem to all of us. That's what we said. We must abide by that.' He waited.

Still Selena and I were silent. She had closed her eyes, tightened her trembling lips. I was silent, at cost of much effort, only because of the pleading look she had given me, a look that willed me not to speak. And then, too, I didn't know how to begin, nor even exactly what to say.

After a moment, he said gently, 'All right, girls. I realize now that it happens sometimes that friends fall out. They say things, do things, that they regret. But, Jennifer, I do think you must learn to curb your temper. It isn't quite ladylike, is it, for girls to be physically aggressive?'

I gasped, 'Dr. Paulen!'

'Hank, if you please,' he smiled, his gleaming eyes cold.

'Hank, you don't think...'

16

Selena cried, 'Oh, no. That isn't it! Jennifer never...'

He held my moccasin out to me. He said, 'I expect you'll need this, Jennifer.'

I thanked him in a shaky voice. I went on, 'But you've completely misunderstood...'

He gave us both a long speculative look. Then he said, 'Suppose the two of you settle on whatever your story will be, and later on we'll discuss it.' With that he left us alone.

CHAPTER TWO

Selena pushed herself out of the chair, took three shaky steps, then sank onto the edge of her bed. 'I wish he hadn't come in just then,' she told me.

'I think we'd better explain what happened,' I answered.

'Oh, no!' She shook her head from side to side, her violet eyes pleading with me again.

'But that's silly, Selena. Why not?'

She didn't answer me.

'Selena, look, he's very ... well, he's a very understanding man, wouldn't you say?'

She whispered, 'I guess he is.'

'Then...'

'I'm afraid,' she said, still whispering.

'Afraid?' I echoed. 'But he won't...'

Her mouth tightened into a rigid pale line.

17

She spat words at me like stones. She said, 'You just don't want him to believe we've had a fight. All right, maybe I don't blame you, but you're just thinking about yourself, about him. Suppose you stop and think of me for a minute.'

'Okay.' I sighed. 'I guess you're partly right anyhow.' I sat on the edge of my bed, facing her.

Everything in the room was doubled: her bed and mine; her desk under the window and mine beside it; two black and red braided oval rugs; two closets; two black and red throws. It should have been a nice room, but there was something stiff and unreal about it. It was hard to believe that the two of us, Selena and I, really lived there. I suppose it was because neither of us had put up pictures, or set out the usual gimcracks or souvenirs. It was as if we knew we'd only come for a little while and didn't intend to stay any longer than we had to.

'I guess you're partly right,' I repeated. 'But only that, Selena. I'm afraid, too. Don't you see that?'

'Something happened to me,' she cried. 'I know it did.' She paused, swallowed. 'I really *know*, you see, but you can't believe me, can you?'

I temporized by saying, 'I know something happened, but I don't know what. And I'm not sure—'

'That's the thing!' she cut in. 'You're not

18

sure, and you were right here. Do you suppose he'll believe me? Do you really suppose he'll understand? He'll just say that I'm crazy, or something like that anyhow. If we tell him, he'll surely think I'm some kind of a nut. Maybe he'll even decide to send me away. And if he did that ... oh, Jennifer, I couldn't stand it. I couldn't stand to have to leave.'

I didn't know what to answer. I let the silence grow between us. I was scared, too. I was just as frightened as Selena was. I had heard her scream, seen her flail at the empty air. I had looked at those terrible scratches on her throat and wrists. Yes, I was frightened, too.

She said at last, 'Maybe it *was* a dream. Maybe I just imagined it.'

I looked pointedly at her throat, and a flush spread over her pale face, then receded, leaving it even more pale than before.

'But you told me I might have dreamed it. You even said ...' Her throat moved as she swallowed with great effort. 'I don't know what to do,' she went on after a moment. Her violet eyes made a slow careful circuit of the room and finally settled on the unused fireplace. She said, her voice trembling, 'Please, Jennifer, just forget it. It must have been a dream. Just a silly crazy dream. Let's not say any more about it. Even if he asks us.'

She rose and briskly turned on the overhead light. As the old chandelier blossomed, the shadows seemed to flee from the room.

19

She gave me a smile that seemed almost normal. 'I'm sorry I threw such a fit. I guess I scared you halfway to death. But it's all over now. Really, Jennifer, it's over.'

Her eyes were almost too bright, and I saw that her hand shook when she reached for her hairbrush. She gave her long tangled hair a single swipe, then put the brush down and stood there, staring at herself in the mirror.

She could say what she wanted about forgetting what had happened, but I knew that she hadn't. She couldn't, and I couldn't either. As I changed into red and black striped hiphuggers and put on a fresh shirt, I thought back over those earlier moments. 'It's the *Group Mind*,' Selena had whispered with anguish in her eyes. 'The *Group Mind*...'

It had sounded like an interesting course when I saw it listed in the school catalogue. I wasn't sure just what my field of interest would finally be, but I was considering psychology, so I judged it could be of value to me later on. Besides, I was attracted to the idea of a seminar. Instead of hearing a lecture, taking notes, sitting shoulder to shoulder among sixty or eighty students, I would be one of a very small number, surely not more than twelve. Instead of lectures there would be discussions. Instead of being graded on exams, the students would be marked in terms of their participation. There were very few seminars open to undergraduate students, and I was curious to see what it would be like. My advisor was less than enthusiastic, but when I insisted, he allowed me to include it in my program, along with English, second-year French, biology, and philosophy.

I went to the first meeting on a crisp sunny early September day. The room was small. A long mahogany table seemed almost to fill it. Heavy arm chairs were set around it, ready to be occupied. The stucco walls were a restful pale green. The single window was long and narrow, allowing in only a thin tunnel of the sunlight that warmed the out of doors. A roll-away blackboard stood nearby. In white chalk was written: Dr. Henry Paulen. Psych. 155. No texts.

I was only moments early, but no one else had arrived. I studied the empty room with a queer quiver of anticipation and interest. It was the first time I had felt that upon beginning any course. Somehow, the year before, in my freshman days, the work had seemed lifeless and dull, the texts unreal. I had managed to do well by memorizing great lists of French verbs and quotations from English poets, but I felt that I had actually learned very little. Now, with a lift of excitement, I began to think that this would be different. It certainly was more different than I could have imagined then, and the lessons I learned in it will follow me, haunt me, for the rest of my life.

As I stood there imagining the great outflow

of knowledge awaiting me, Dr. Paulen came in.

I was instantly charmed. He seemed to be in his midforties, but lean and graceful. His dark beard was small and carefully trimmed. His gleaming dark eyes examined me with a look of approval. He spoke, 'Early, aren't you?'

I nodded. 'I'm Jennifer Alton.'

'I'm glad to have you with us, Jennifer.' He nodded toward a chair. 'Have a seat.'

I sat down, arranged my books and papers before me.

He smiled faintly. He took the chair at the head of the table and pulled a pipe from his pocket and lit it.

I was watching and our glances met over the flickering match. I found myself blinking, looking away quickly.

His eyes were very bright with a glittering blackness like that of rain-washed coal which shone from beneath long dark lashes. His nose was high bridged, with flaring nostrils. The dark beard and mustache seemed to narrow and lengthen his face. His dark hair was longish but carefully cut and brushed. He wore a black turtleneck sweater and black trousers. A small gold emblem of some sort winked at me from the roll of his sweater.

I fiddled with my pencils and wished I could think of something to say as the silence between us grew longer and longer. That had always been one of my troubles, I realized. I could never really talk to any of the professors.

They all seemed so old to me, so distant and reserved. I didn't know how to use words to bridge the separation.

Then Dr. Paulen said, 'This is going to be a somewhat unusual course, Jennifer. I hope that you're prepared for that and willing to go along with it.'

'I hope so too.' I glanced toward him, and again our eyes met. I found myself thinking that he was the handsomest man I had ever seen in my life and wished I had worn something more interesting than my old blue jeans. Immediately I could feel a blush burn in my cheeks.

He smiled faintly again and I had the terrible feeling that he knew exactly what I was thinking, but he said, 'I believe you're probably quite ready. You seem mature enough. What do you plan for your major?'

'I've decided on psychology,' I told him, certain suddenly that the decision troubling me for the past year troubled me no longer. I would go into psychology and get my degree and maybe, some day, like Dr. Paulen, I would have a Ph.D. I grinned, almost light-headed with relief, and blurted out, 'But I only just decided.' He grinned back at me through the haze of smoke from his pipe and I felt the blush burn in my cheeks once more.

'Let's hope you don't change your mind,' he said.

'Oh, I won't,' I promised fervently. 'I'm sure

that I won't. Not any more.' But I didn't know then what I was promising myself and him.

At that moment, there was a surge of movement at the door. I felt a quick flare of disappointment. I wished that my time alone with him could have gone on and on. It was the first of many times that I had that same feeling. However, at the same time, I was relieved by the interruption. I had had the strange and uncomfortable sensation that he was carefully assessing me, feeling me out, studying my thoughts and reactions. I reminded myself that he was a psychologist and that he probably did that with everyone he met, by habit as well as interest. But just the same I felt better when his attention was diverted from me by the entrance of the others.

They bunched in the doorway together, laughing, and talking, until Dr. Paulen rose, said, 'Come in,' and went on to introduce himself.

Selena Sellers was the first to enter the room. Her hair was blonde and shining, almost to her waist, and tied back in a bright red ribbon. Later, when she began to change, I remember how carefully groomed she was that morning, even though she was as casually dressed, in a blue shirt and white trousers, as the rest of us were. Her violet eyes touched Dr. Paulen, lingered for a moment, so that I knew she was noting his good looks. Then she gave me a sweet, dreamy smile and sat down beside me, murmuring her name softly.

Don Reagon followed her. He was short and lanky. His hair was sandy and hung to his shoulders but was clean and neat. He wore a blue sweat shirt and black slacks. I guessed he was nineteen, and later on found out I was right. He took a chair at the table without saying anything.

'Your name?' Dr. Paulen asked, his silky voice quivering through me suddenly.

Don told him, then leaned back, closing his hazel eyes. It was some time before I learned that Don was the only son of Jared Reagon, a world-famous criminal lawyer, and it wasn't Don, but one of the others, that told me.

Dr. Paulen studied him thoughtfully for a long moment, then shrugged and turned away as Jimbill Desiral and Victor Tarnaby came in together.

Jimbill was tall and very thin, with a narrow aristocratic face and brilliant blue eyes. His blond hair was wavy but short. I noticed all that in a single glance and knew that Selena had, too, for she suddenly straightened up in her seat, that dreamy smile curving her lips. I had known him for several weeks before I learned that he was a junior, was twenty years old, and the son of a very well-known and high-born Southern family that was now completely penniless. When I knew that I understood better his calm exterior and perfect manners, first exhibited in the way he introduced himself to Dr. Paulen, then to Selena and me, and finally to Don Reagon, before he took his chair.

Victor Tarnaby was much more casual. I recognized his background at a glance, because, I suppose, it was so much like my own. He was eighteen, too, and a redhead. His eyes were an alert pale green. He had very endearing dimples, and I guessed that he hated them. He wore a wrinkled and torn shirt, dirty bell-bottom pants and badly worn sneakers. From knowing about my own parents, I knew about his. His father was self-made and proud of it. His mother was just getting used to the idea that she had made it into the middle class suburbs with her husband. Victor was brilliant but didn't have any goals, I suspected. It surprised me, when I knew him better, how close to the truth I was, yet how wrong I was, too.

Mike Justin was next. He was nineteen, muscular, and very broad shouldered. He wore a T-shirt boasting the university name and walked like a wrestler. It didn't surprise me at all to find out that he was on an athletic scholarship and was taking the course because he thought it was good for a passing grade, no matter how little he worked. He had brown hair and a rugged brown face. His gray eyes were set deep under a ridged brow. He told us his name in a rough, gravelly voice, and sprawled in the chair next to Selena. She immediately straightened up again.

The girl who followed him in was beautiful. There was no other way to describe her. She had golden hair and wide smoky blue eyes. Her chin was pointed and her cheekbones high. Her body was voluptuously curved, but she walked as if she were completely unaware of it. She wore a dress, snug at the waist and sleeveless, in royal blue. It floated around her as she drifted in, smiled at Dr. Paulen, then at the rest of us, and murmured, 'I'm Harriet Varnum, and I know this is going to be fun.'

The last person to enter was Bess Ardway. She had short curly auburn hair and deep brown eyes. Her complexion was creamy satin. Her body was slightly plump, but curved prettily. She wore an expensive pantsuit and a golden charm bracelet that tinkled as she put her books on the table and took a chair. In a quick, no-nonsense voice she introduced herself and then sat back with an air of waiting to be shown.

'We're here,' Dr. Paulen said after a moment's silence, 'to study the Group Mind. That is, to try to understand and perhaps develop, some new ideas about why people welded into units, groups, segments of society, are able to do things that they might not, as individuals, be able to do.' He paused, and Mike Justin sighed and wriggled in his seat.

Dr. Paulen smiled faintly, then went on, 'We know, already, that such is the case. It is a phenomenon that has been observed thousands of times through history, and in our own years as well. Now can anyone give me some examples of what I mean to start us off?'

There was a small silence. Then Bess Ardway tilted her auburn head forward. Her deep brown eyes rested on Dr. Paulen. She asked, 'What about lynchings? What about vigilante groups?'

Jimbill's bright blue eyes were serious. He said, 'Wait a minute. What are you talking about lynchings for?'

Dr. Paulen intervened. 'I think it's a fairly good example of mob psychology, don't you? And vigilante groups as well.'

'Maybe,' Jimbill drawled, but reluctantly.

'No maybes,' Bess said firmly. 'Maybe you don't like the idea, but we're here to learn, not necessarily to like.'

Once again, Dr. Paulen intervened. He said, 'What we must try to learn is how it happens, what actually occurs, what forces are responsible. Does anybody have any ideas?'

No one spoke. There was a rustle of uneasiness at the long table.

I glanced up and met Don Reagon's hazel eyes.

Dr. Paulen said, 'We must consider all the possibilities, you know. Is there something, an entity, which we can fairly call the Group Mind?'

Possibilities ... an entity called the Group

Mind...

That was the moment it began; that was the way—

I was suddenly aware of Selena's voice saying, 'Jennifer, Jennifer, what's the matter with you? Why are you just sitting there like that? There's the dinner bell. Can't you hear it?'

I came back to the present with a start, glad to be recalled from that first day in the seminar. I didn't want to think about it any more, nor to remember what had followed.

'Yes,' I said quickly. 'I did hear it, and we'd better go. I'm all ready. Are you?'

She had, I saw, never finished brushing her hair, but she had put rouge on her cheeks, and now it stood out in two garish circles under her shadowed eyes.

She took two steps toward the door, then stopped.

'I don't want to go down.'

'You'd better. You ought to eat something.'

'I can't.'

'If you don't, Dr. Paulen's going to know something is really wrong, Selena.'

Terror was evident in her face. She murmured,

'Something is.'

'I know. But still...'

'I can't sit there and pretend. Not now. Not yet.'

'Selena,' my voice shook, and I paused to try

to steady it, to make it firm and reasonable, to make it sound more sure than I really felt. 'Selena,' I repeated finally, 'we'll figure out what happened. We just won't say anything, and maybe he'll forget about it. And the others ... they won't know. Don't worry about it. We'll just ignore the whole thing.'

She cried, 'Oh, dear God, don't you see? They have to know. It's not just me, Jennifer. What about you? What about the rest of the kids? Don't you understand that it could happen to any of us?'

I didn't understand. What was she talking about? Why did she think something would happen to the rest of us? Surely her own vulnerability had led her to imagine an attack that had never occurred. It must be that. It had to be.

But something in me whispered, *The scratches? Her terror? No one was here. No one was on the stairs.*

I said, 'I don't know what you're talking about, but I do know we've got to get down there, Selena.'

She gave me a wan smile and opened the door. 'I guess I don't know what I'm talking about either.' Her tone told me that she was making a valiant effort to fight off her fear, to pretend now that nothing had happened to her that evening in the twilight-filled room.

As I went to the door, I saw a glint in the corner near the desk. I don't know why I did it, but I went over to see what it was. When I did, leaning over, I repressed a gasp. A sharp-pointed nailfile lay there, shining in the light from the chandelier. I picked it up, turned it in my fingers.

'What's that?' Selena asked.

I held it out to her wordlessly.

She stared at it but didn't touch it. Immediately she understood the thought passing through my mind. She said, as if the words were wrenched from her unwilling throat, 'No, Jennifer. I swear to you. I didn't scratch myself with that. I swear I didn't. I couldn't have. And why should I lie? Why should I lie about it?'

I dropped the file on her desk and shrugged. 'Oh, never mind. Let's just go down to dinner now.'

I didn't believe her. Poor Selena. Nobody listened. Nobody believed. Nobody understood. Not until it was too late...

CHAPTER THREE

The others were all at the table.

It was long and dark, almost a replica of the one in our classroom on campus, but the chairs set around it were straight, padded with a musty and worn fabric of woven black and red.

The walls were a dark paneled wood and

31

scattered on them were a child's drawings, a tilted tree, a falling-down house, a three-legged bear, all framed in elaborately carved wood and painted gold. They had been done, Dr. Paulen told me, by his son many years before.

I felt then that I could not ask him about his son, about his wife. Something in his face had warned me not to. But now, looking at the child's drawings, I found myself wondering about the boy, about his mother. It was the first time I had thought of them since I asked Dr. Paulen about the drawings.

A Tiffany shade covered the overhead light, casting a blue green shadow on us all. Selena hesitated in the doorway. I gave her a reassuring touch, and she moved forward, her steps soundless on the heavy dark green carpet. She slipped into her seat, smiling faintly. I followed her.

Dr. Paulen looked at her, then at me. 'All right now?'

'Yes,' I said quickly.

Selena nodded her head.

'What's wrong?' Jimbill asked, brilliant blue eyes fixed on Selena's face.

'Nothing,' I told him. 'Nothing at all.'

'Then why didn't you get the table set?' Bess demanded. She tossed her auburn head, and the light of battle appeared in her deep brown eyes. 'It was your day to do the table, and you know it, Jennifer.'

I had completely forgotten about it.

32

Somehow, from the moment I entered the house that evening, I had left behind me the reality of chores. I said contritely, 'I'm sorry. It slipped my mind.'

'Oh, you just forgot, so Harriet and I had to do it. Along with the cooking. It's not fair for us to get stuck with everything.'

'It's my fault,' Selena said quietly. 'I got her distracted, and—'

'Okay, okay,' Harriet cut in with an appeasing laugh. 'What difference does it make? Tomorrow Selena and Jennifer can cook and set the table and then we'll all be square again.'

Selena gave her a grateful smile, and I nodded my agreement.

'No need to make a federal case,' she went on. 'We have plenty to eat, haven't we? And a warm place to stay? And whatever we want. That's what I tell my sister and brother when they start fighting. It doesn't make sense to make a federal case.'

Nobody answered. I knew just what was passing through the minds of the others. There went Harriet, twenty years old, a sexpot if there ever was one, talking about her family again, showing off her hunger for home that embarrassed us all.

Jimbill started passing the platters around. When we had served ourselves, and settled down to eat, Dr. Paulen glanced at me. The gold emblem winked at me from the roll of his

33

turtleneck sweater. I suddenly realized that he wore it almost all the time. Or was it all the time? I tried to avoid his eyes. I choked down a mouthful of spaghetti and concentrated on my plate.

He said in his slow silky voice, 'I came upon an odd scene this morning,' and waited.

Selena and I were obviously expected to react. We did. She moved in her chair, and I forked more spaghetti into my mouth.

'There's been plenty of odd things,' Don said, with a flick of hazel eyes in my direction.

He said aloud what I was thinking silently as I let my glance slip cautiously around the table. It seemed to me that we had all changed in the two months since September. Everyone of us had been marked in some peculiar way by the seminar.

Mike's hard brown face seemed to have paled. Now, instead of rushing out to football practice or to games with gusto and anticipation, he went reluctantly. And he came limping back, more and more frequently, with tape on his face and bruised hands.

Victor's green eyes seemed less bright and direct, and he had developed a slight stutter that slowed his speech, and made him blush until his face seemed aflame.

Don had become more quiet, less sure of himself. He often appeared distracted, as if he were listening to some sound I couldn't hear, or waiting for something to happen that I couldn't know about.

Thinner than ever now, Jimbill had developed a slouch, and his slow drawl had become even more pronounced.

There were deep dark shadows under Harriet's smoky blue eyes, and her golden hair had dulled. Her infectious giggle sounded shrill to me now.

Bess's curved and sexy plumpness was less attractive somehow, and her brisk manner softened. A strange nervousness possessed her, so that she fidgeted in class and paced the floor of her room.

I wasn't sure that I could see myself as clearly as I could see the others, but my eyes did seem bigger, my face paler. I knew that I felt tension, even fear. I didn't know just where it came from.

However, I was sure that of all of us, Selena had been the most affected. Dreamy, poetic Selena, who had notebooks full of her writing but hadn't added to them recently, seemed to have fallen into a well of terror and been marked by it.

Even then, that night, as I looked around the dinner table at the others, I saw what was happening. But it was only the beginning...

We had started out in the seminar by discussing the aspects of mob psychology that were the most obvious. From that early discussion we came upon the idea that perhaps out of the interaction of people in a group,

35

some new element was formed, an element that existed on its own once born, able to act by itself, without direction or control by the individuals who had conceived it.

I remember that Bess had objected to the concept at first. 'Oh, no,' she said. 'It couldn't act independently. Those who had created it would be able to stop it if they wanted to.'

Don disagreed, 'Why? After all, a man and a woman come together and produce a child. A part of each of them is in that child, but the child is separate from them, and distinctly its own person. Couldn't it be like that?'

'We have to consider both angles,' Dr. Paulen said, but I felt that he was pleased by what Don had proposed.

Later, we all somehow found ourselves in agreement. A mob, on its own, produces a mind: the Group Mind. It can function, and does, without the direct participation of the individuals who created it. From there it was an easy and obvious next step to decide to try the experiments which finally excited us all so much. We decided we would attempt to invoke a Group Mind, the product of our eight minds, working with Dr. Paulen in the class. We began a series of concentration tests, experimental playlets, designed by the seminar as a whole, in an attempt to raise this new entity.

I became gradually aware of an increasing uneasiness. I didn't like the idea of some of the experiments. I didn't like the stress we all placed on the uncontrollability of the Group Mind. I kept having the feeling, never quite put into words, that we were somehow dealing in black magic, in what must be forbidden. We were attempting what should not even be attempted. I couldn't explain it, not even to myself. I certainly didn't know how to talk about it in words.

I did try though. When I went home on the bus in early October, just seventy miles from campus, I told my father about the seminar. I described its goals and techniques.

He sipped his bourbon on the rocks, looked at his watch, and said, 'I guess that's how the colleges are going these days. Colleges and everything else. It's the damndest thing, Jennifer, how they insist on wasting time. But don't worry about it. Stick it out. You'll be okay. Get what you can out of that junk, and forget the rest.' A few minutes later, he went out to play golf.

I told myself that I oughtn't to blame him. I hadn't really explained how I felt. Maybe describing the course wasn't enough. I wished he had really been listening to me. I wished he had paid as much attention to me then as he paid to the stock market quotations in the morning papers. He didn't need a detailed explanation to understand them.

Most of that weekend my mother was busy with preparing for her bridge club. While I helped her set up the tables, I told her a little bit about Dr. Paulen. 'He sounds very attractive,' she said. 'Don't you dare get a crush on him. There's nothing sillier than an eighteen year old mooning over some old man.'

'He's only in his forties,' I had answered, 'and that's not really what I'm talking about. It's the class. It...'

'Are you already flunking out?' she demanded. Then, 'Don't you dare. Your father would have a fit. He's bound and determined that his only daughter get her college degree. Now me, I don't think it's all that important, but he does. So...'

I finally managed to cut in with, 'I don't think I'm failing. It's nothing like that.'

She chuckled, 'Your trouble is your imagination, Jennifer. It is now, and it always has been. Now, run in and see if the mold is firming up, and forget your seminar and your Dr. Paulen, and your silly crush on him.'

I wondered if it was my imagination that made me feel that neither of my parents had really been listening to me. Later that day, though, I made one more effort. Afterward, I wished I hadn't. When I saw Abel Harding pull into his driveway down the block, I waited a few minutes, and then, without telling my mother, I went down to his house.

I'd known Abel all my life it seemed to me. We'd managed to be good friends, even though he was seven years older, for as long as I could remember.

He had always had time to answer my questions. He had always managed to be around to pick me up when I fell. I had always thought of him as confidante and protector and the source of all wisdom. Within the last few years a peculiar gap had developed between us, however. I was uncomfortably aware of how frequently he treated me like a child. It annoyed me that he didn't realize that I was completely grown up and that I had caught up with him now. That he could treat me as an equal. I didn't let that keep me from going to see him because I refused to allow that small annoyance to interfere with what had been the habit of a lifetime. When I was troubled I went to Abel. I did that then.

He was sitting on his back patio sipping a drink, and squinting thoughtfully at his cigarette. He had dark curly hair, cut very short, and clear cool blue eyes. His mouth was long and narrow, and fell easily into a wide warm grin. He had a wiry build, long legs, and big square hands. He was a newspaperman, and affected casual dress. That day he wore an open-necked shirt, a red pullover vest, and dark gray trousers.

He gave me a wide smile. 'So the prodigal returns. How come? I thought you were so anxious to get the term started we wouldn't see you until the summer recess.'

'I wanted to see what was going on at home,' I told him.

He gestured to a chair. 'If you're as tired as I am, you'll want to sit down.'

I lowered myself into the canvasback, asked, 'What are *you* so tired from?'

'Chasing a story that won't jell,' he answered, sipping at his drink.

I didn't much care for liquor, but I stared pointedly at his glass. He ignored the look.

I sighed, asked, 'What's the story about?'

'Municipal corruption, if you must know.'

'I guess it's secret stuff.'

'You guess right. But that's only because so far it's only my intuition that I've got to go on. I trust my feelings, you know, Jennifer. My work keeps teaching me that over and over again. When I get the proof, and I will, you better believe me, I will use it. The editor has already given me his word, so . . .' Abel grinned then. 'The trouble is that feelings aren't proof, and I've got to dig for that.'

'Feelings aren't proof,' I repeated, thinking of the seminar and Dr. Paulen.

He gave me a sharp look, put his glass on a tiled table. 'That's not such a good phrase that it's worth saying twice. Especially not in that tone of voice. What's on your mind, Jennifer?' It was just like years before. Abel sensing my problem, leaning forward to listen to me.

I folded my hands in my lap to keep them from trembling. I ignored the flush of embarrassment on my cheeks. I tried to put sensibly and coolly into words my feeling

40

about the seminar. He listened without comment, his big hands on his knees, his clear blue eyes attentive.

When I was finished, I sat back, relieved. Abel, I was sure, would know what I ought to do. Abel, I was certain, would understand what troubled me. Always, always, he had known the answers to my questions. He would surely know the answer to this one, too. But, after a moment's silence, he threw back his dark head and laughed and reached for a cigarette, and I felt frozen, diminished, suddenly a child again.

Over the flaring match, he asked, 'Just how far do you think you have to go to justify your boredom, Jennifer?'

I stared at him. 'What?'

'Boredom, I said.' He had stopped laughing by then. He went on seriously, 'Now, look. I don't think a course in mob psychology should be taught that way, except perhaps as a means to encourage independent thinking. This is certainly something new. Go along with it. It makes you uncomfortable, you say. I think you're bored with it and building up some sweet imaginative supernatural deal just to keep yourself on your toes.'

'But I'm not,' I protested. 'Abel, listen. I have French and English and biology, and philosophy, as well as the seminar. I'm having a terribly hard time concentrating on any of them. I don't have time to be bored. It can't be

41

that.'

He shook his head. 'You know just as well as I do, and you'll admit it if you're honest, that you're just fed up with school, and looking for a good excuse to drop out, and I wish you wouldn't. I wish you'd stick it out. In another few months you'll feel entirely differently.'

'But that isn't it, Abel,' I objected, trying to ignore his soothing big brother tone, but feeling my temper begin to rise. 'It's just that I get the willies from that particular class and from Dr. Paulen, too. I can't explain it. It just happens. I think the material is interesting enough, but I just have the feeling...'

'You didn't want to go back to school this term,' he reminded me soberly.

It was true that I hadn't. I wished he didn't feel it necessary to remind me of that just then. He didn't know my reason. I hadn't been particularly stimulated in my first year. Yes, that was part of it. The real thing, though, was that I hadn't wanted to leave him. I had missed him terribly the winter before and I didn't want to go through that again. My father had insisted, so I had gone, with Abel's persuasion to buoy me up.

'But I did go,' I said finally. 'And I took the seminar, and Dr. Paulen.'

'Dr. Paulen ...' Abel said thoughtfully. 'I know that name. I can't remember the connection in which I heard it, but I'm sure I have heard it.'

42

Abel's mother came out to the patio then. She carried a tray, and put it down next to me, patting my long hair. 'I thought it was about time for some milk and cookies for you, Jennifer. It's nice to have you hanging around again.'

I thought disconsolately that she was just as bad as Abel. They both insisted on thinking of me as if I were twelve years old. Couldn't they see that I had changed? What was wrong with them? I nibbled a cookie, gulped the milk down.

When Abel's mother went into the house he got to his feet. 'Look, I've got some work to do now, and I have to be back at the paper in a couple of hours.' His blue eyes didn't quite meet mine. I knew he wasn't telling me the truth. He just wanted to get rid of me.

I got up quickly. 'Sorry, Abel. I'll be on my way.'

His hands dropped lightly to cup my shoulders. 'Hold on a minute. I've got something more to say. I hope you'll make the effort to get over the boredom bit, and I want you to promise me something. Will you?'

'Sure. But what?'

'Just stick to it, Jennifer. Don't trick yourself into doing anything so foolish as to drop out of that class because a) you either don't like it; or b) because you're scared of it, and I want you to promise you won't fake yourself into dropping out of school, too.'

43

It was maddening that he insisted on forcing what I had told him to fit his preconceived idea. It was maddening that he didn't see me as I was now. Years before I would have thrown a temper tantrum. Now all I could say was, 'You just don't understand, Abel.'

'I understand only too well. I haven't been out of college all that long myself, you know,' he answered. 'Now: promise, Jennifer.'

After a long hesitation, I said unwillingly, 'Okay, Abel. If that's what you want, then I'll stick it out. Both the seminar and school.'

'That's what I want.'

'Okay.' I turned away, unsatisfied and disappointed.

I started down the driveway and when I reached the road, I looked back. Abel was still outside. He had come from the back patio, stood near the garage, watching me as I walked away. He lifted his hand in a wave, and I saw the flash of his smile, before I turned into the street.

I went back to school the next morning. I told myself that maybe Abel was right. The whole thing was something I had cooked up in my mind because the seminar was unorthodox. I told myself I would stick it out, as I'd promised him, no matter what.

It was then that I learned that Dr. Paulen had a house on Dandy Lane, and that Jimbill had already moved into it.

Jimbill told me about it, his brilliant blue

eyes aglow. 'Mike and I went down there yesterday, and it's really something. Big, you know? Lots and lots of rooms. Really, a mob could get lost in that place, and plenty of privacy, quiet for studying. Then, you want to hear the wildest thing? Dr. Paulen asked Mike and me if we wanted to move in. Rent free! I jumped at it.' Jimbill grinned. 'You bet I did. The family plantation is run down to nothing, and so is the bank account. And living rent free ... well, you wouldn't know it, Jennifer. But it'll make all the difference to me.'

I said slowly, 'I guess it will, Jimbill.'

'So I moved in last night.' His thin face sobered. 'The only thing is, it's awfully quiet. I mean, that's good for studying, but the rest of the time, you know?'

'What about Mike? Didn't he move in, too?'

'He's going to think it over. I'll bet he goes along. Free rent! After all, he's scrounging for pennies just like me.'

Jimbill was right. Mike moved in the following afternoon. By the end of the week Victor and Don had joined them, and Saturday night, the four boys and Dr. Paulen invited us to dinner. It was festive with candlelight and wine.

Dr. Paulen smiled at me, said silkily, 'What we really need here is a woman's touch, or four women's touch, I should say.' He surveyed the hamburgers, the baked potatoes, on the table. 'We're going to get tired of this simple fare.'

'Is there room?' Selena asked, her dreamy eyes fixed on Jimbill.

'Of course,' Dr. Paulen answered, 'and I am a very adequate chaperone.'

Selena looked at me. I didn't say anything. She looked at Harriet.

Harriet giggled. 'If you're asking me with your eyes what I think you're asking, then the answer is okay. Why not?'

'Suppose the two of us moved in?' Selena asked.

Dr. Paulen nodded solemnly. 'Of course. You're all welcome. This is a big house, and I'm happy to have company.'

Bess and I still said nothing.

The next day Harriet explained, 'It's more like home to me, Jennifer. I mean a house and all that. I don't care about the dorm or school either. I never did. I got terrible grades in high school, and three colleges turned me down, so I spent a year at home. You know me. I'm on the boy bit. My father wrangled a place for me here last year and he wants me to stay. I mean, what else does a girl do until she gets married, you know? Only I'm so homesick for my brother and sister. The family, the living together ... oh, this will be much better for me.'

Within a few days, Bess joined the others. 'I don't like being an outsider,' is all she told me in explanation.

I didn't like being an outsider either, but I was the only one who stayed in the dorm.

That lasted only a few weeks though. In some way not clear to me, the seminar group ended up spending all its time together. We separated for our other classes, of course, but our work and study always drew us back together. Our social lives revolved more and more around the house on Dandy Lane. Even though I stayed on at the dorm, I found myself only sleeping there, while the rest of my time I was with the others in the group. It became so obvious that my dorm roommate, Helen Byers, asked irritably, 'What do you see in those kooks anyway? If you see so much in them why do you bother hanging around here?'

That was just what Selena and Harriet kept asking me. Why did I stay in the dorm? Why didn't I move in with them? I didn't know the answer myself. I just felt uneasy about it, about the house on Dandy Lane, about Dr. Paulen. I finally wrote to my folks, hoping that they would resolve my dilemma by forbidding me to leave the dorm. My mother wrote back that I could do whatever I wanted to do, but still I hesitated for two days before I moved in with the others.

As soon as I did I felt that strange mixture of repulsion and attraction that had assailed me ever since. I couldn't walk up the gravel road without feeling it. I couldn't even think of that gray toad of a house without feeling it.

Gradually the others paired off: Selena and

Jimbill; Harriet and Mike; Bess and Victor. Only Don and I held ourselves aloof—or tried to. It hadn't been easy on us. We hadn't been successful either.

Often Dr. Paulen would say, 'We all live together. I feel that we're friends. I think you should call me Hank. At least while we're at home.'

I found that very hard to do, although I could feel myself being drawn to him more and more, while my uneasiness grew more and more, too.

Now, sitting at the dinner table, seeing how all the others had changed, knowing that I, too, had changed, remembering Selena's awful screams in our room, I heard Bess repeat Dr. Paulen's words: 'You came upon an odd scene? What do you mean, Hank?'

The slow careful way in which she spoke startled me. She didn't sound like herself. She sounded like a parrot repeating a phrase that it had been taught to say, a phrase without meaning.

Selena grew smaller in her chair. Her mouth tightened. I slid a glance at Dr. Paulen.

He was smiling. His dark eyes gleamed. He said, 'I suppose, since neither Jennifer nor Selena seem willing to discuss it, I must do so myself.' He paused, plainly waiting. Then, 'I'd sooner one of you girls brought it out into the open.'

Selena took a loud gulping breath. 'Listen,'

48

she said in a quick hard voice. 'Listen, it was just absolutely nothing. Private business. Nothing. Honest, Hank. There's no need to make anything of it.'

His straight dark brows rose. His smile broadened within his beard. 'Nothing?' he repeated. He looked at the others. 'I came into the house, and was greeted by Selena's voice. She was in her room, screaming—screaming terribly. I raced up the steps, and lying there, on one of them, was a moccasin I recognized as Jennifer's. I hurried up into their room, and the girls—'

'It was just a dream,' Selena cried hoarsely, and burst into tears.

The others stared at her. Then Jimbill pushed back his chair and got up. He went to her, took her hand. 'Hey, honey, nobody goes all to pieces over a bad dream. You come on along with me. Let's just go talk about it.'

She jerked her hand from his, shuddering away from his touch.

He drawled, smiling, his blue eyes anxious, 'It's just me, honey, old Jimbill. Don't carry on that way now. We'll fix it for you. Whatever it is, we'll fix it.'

Dr. Paulen said silkily, 'It's in your hands, isn't it, Jennifer?'

I looked first at Selena, then at him. I didn't know what to say.

'If you won't tell us ...' he began.

I said quickly, 'I don't know what happened
49

actually. I came in, just the way you did. I heard Selena screaming and ran up into the room. Nobody was there. Nothing was wrong. She was just on the floor, screaming and crying.'

'And ...' Dr. Paulen prompted me.

I looked at him blankly.

'So you scratched her throat and arms? To make her stop screaming perhaps?'

'I did not!' I cried. 'Ask Selena!'

He transferred his dark gaze to her white face. 'Well?'

'No. She didn't,' Selena whispered. 'I just got the scratches. I don't know how.'

'You don't know how?' he asked softly.

She shook her head.

I thought of the nailfile that had been lying in the corner. Could she have used that on herself? But why? Why? Was it possible that she had done it without knowing it? Again, why—And how was it possible?

'The scratches just came of their own accord, that's what you want us to believe?' Dr. Paulen persisted.

Again she shook her head.

He sighed, looked around the table. 'Does that seem likely to you?'

One by one they shook their heads in the negative.

I was the only one who didn't agree. I simply sat there, shivering. I wondered why he was so insistent. Why wouldn't he forget it? What did he want of Selena, of me?

'Selena?' he asked.

She straightened up, shoved back her chair. She got to her feet.

I knew, even before she spoke, what she would say. I knew how far he had forced her.

She said, 'All right, all right. I'll say it then. I'll tell you so you can laugh at me. It was the Group Mind that did it. The Group Mind!'

Strangely, no one gasped, spoke, demurred.

Dr. Paulen smiled in his beard. Then he said gravely, 'Good for you, Selena. At least you're being honest with yourself, with us, in what you believe.' He spread another look around the table. 'Of course, that doesn't mean that the rest of us quite understand your accusation, or agree with it either. But now that you've come out with it, I'm sure I can help you.'

CHAPTER FOUR

She fled from the room without answering.

When her footsteps had faded away along the upper hallway, Dr. Paulen said, 'I think, if this should happen again, or anything remotely like it, you must take Selena in to see Dr. Barodini.'

I looked at him blankly.

'Dr. Nancy Barodini,' Dr. Paulen said.

'She's the campus psychiatrist. She's quite adept with undergraduate trauma. I'm sure she can straighten Selena out with no trouble at all.'

I didn't answer him. I couldn't understand his reaction. We, in the seminar, had been trying to raise something we called the Group Mind. We presumably believed that we could do it. Now Selena had said that we had, and his response was to call her ill.

'I expect,' he went on, 'that she's taken our course somewhat too literally. That happens occasionally to an immature person.'

But weren't we supposed to take the course literally? I asked myself. If not, then how were we to take it?

There was no answer in me to my bewilderment. I knew something was wrong with Selena, something badly wrong. I was frightened of the thought of taking her to a psychiatrist. I didn't know how she would react. I knew only that I wanted her to awaken in the morning her sweet dreamy self again, with the scratches healed. None of the others seemed to take what she had said seriously.

Jimbill said, 'I guess maybe she's been studying too hard. You know how Selena is. She just pushes herself. You'd think her life depended on her grades, and it doesn't. She just doesn't realize...'

Bess said, 'She always struck me as unstable.'

'Oh no,' Harriet protested. 'She's not unstable, but she's like my sister. She gets ideas, you know. Ideas...'

But then Don said quietly, 'Maybe we've done it and don't know it and don't want to believe it.'

'Done what?' Dr. Paulen asked.

'Raised the Group Mind,' Don retorted.

Dr. Paulen laughed softly, 'Do you think it's really possible?'

His laughter was the key. The others instantly followed, hooting with glee at the thought.

Victor nearly fell off his chair, howling, 'Oh, boy, w-w-wouldn't that be-be great?'

Harriet muttered, 'Just ideas, honestly, that's all it is.'

Bess grinned, 'She's been acting funny for a while, hasn't she?'

Don looked at Dr. Paulen. 'If you don't believe it can be done, then why are we trying it, Hank?'

'In order to learn,' Dr. Paulen answered quietly.

Don sank back, a sheepish expression on his face.

That was how the Group Mind was dismissed by the seminar that was supposedly engaged in raising and studying it.

Dr. Paulen looked at me again. 'Remember, Jennifer. I want you to watch Selena. If they should happen again, this kind of a seizure, I mean, you must do as I say.'

I nodded.

'She might need help desperately. We wouldn't want to allow anything to happen to her,' he went on.

Jimbill said suddenly, 'Oh, it won't happen again. I know old Selena. She'll be okay tomorrow, and laughing about the whole thing.'

Maybe he believed it. Maybe it was wishful thinking. I didn't know. But Jimbill was wrong. He was so terribly wrong.

*   *   *

It took such an effort for me to force myself to brush my hair. I leaned against the peeling bathroom wall, and made myself raise the brush, pull it through the long tangled strands.

I felt so tired and down. I wished I didn't have to go to class, but I knew that I had cut English twice already. One more time meant trouble. I had to save that one more time for a real emergency, not waste it because I had slept too heavily to awaken feeling right.

Only moments before, the others had left the house. I had heard them going and leaned from the window. It was another cold cloudy day. They moved in a group down the circular gravel road toward Dandy Lane. Beyond, where the boulevard began, there appeared to be sunlight. I watched them go and wondered what they were thinking, what they were remembering of the evening before.

Selena had been fast asleep when I got up. I decided not to awaken her. She had been so exhausted that she'd fallen into a deep unmoving sleep the moment she slipped into bed.

I had tried to talk to her a little before that, but she shrugged irritably, said, 'Never mind, Jennifer. Let's just forget it, shall we?'

I hoped that Jimbill was right. Maybe it was something she'd gotten out of her system. Maybe it would never happen again.

When the others disappeared into the lane, Dr. Paulen's dark head in their midst, I dragged myself into the shower, hoping that the cold spray would make me feel better. Then, when I had dried and powdered, I set out again to do something about my hair. But every brush stroke was an effort still. I finally gave up, and swept it back off my shoulders. I rubbed powder on my shiny nose and then climbed into my jeans and shirt. I was just putting on my moccasins when I heard Selena cry, 'Jennifer! Jennifer, help me!'

I reached the bedroom in two long jumps. Selena was on the floor, writhing in a blood-stained sheet. Her face was distorted, mouth and eyes wide. Her screams were deafening, horrible to hear.

I pulled the sheet away from her and grabbed her by the shoulders, trying to hold her convulsing body. She rolled away from me, curled into a tight fetal crouch, but in the instant it took her to do that, I saw the new scratches on her thighs. I tried to think where I had last seen the nailfile, but I couldn't remember. I tried to think what to do, but I just didn't know.

I knelt over her, whispering, 'Selena, it's all right. I'm here. Be quiet. Rest now. I'll get help. Selena ... please...'

I don't know if she heard me and understood. But after a few moments had passed, she suddenly went still, relaxed. Her violet eyes opened, and she stared at me in obvious terror.

She whispered shakily, 'Jennifer, don't tell. Remember what Dr. Paulen said.'

'Never mind him. Just think of yourself. You know what we have to do.'

'No!' Her eyes filled with tears. 'Oh, no.'

'I'm going to take you to Dr. Barodini,' I answered. 'Selena, I have to. We have to find out what's wrong and find out what to do.'

'It was another dream,' she said.

'It wasn't, Selena,' I answered as gently as I knew how. 'It couldn't have been. You told me, and the others, just last night that—'

'I was faking it, Jennifer. It was a dream, I tell you!'

I looked, without speaking, at the fresh scratches on her legs.

She jerked the sheet over them. 'I must have

56

done it myself, Jennifer. Please! Can't you see? I just must have!'

'But...'

'I don't want ... I'm afraid...'

I didn't answer her. I gathered her clothes and handed them to her. She dressed slowly and painfully. She shook her hair back from her face, and I asked myself when I had last seen her brush it, tie it in one of those bright ribbons she used to wear.

I started for the door.

'Your books,' she said.

'I'm cutting class this morning, and so are you.'

'Jennifer! I can't! You mustn't!'

We went around and around it, but I wouldn't give in, I couldn't give in. Selena had to have help. I knew I must see that she got it. I didn't want the responsibility, but it was mine, and I had to live up to it.

Finally, protesting all the way, she went with me to the Campus Health Center. I gave her name to the nurse and explained that Selena wanted to see Dr. Nancy Barodini as soon as possible.

The nurse wanted an explanation. Selena wouldn't speak for herself. I finally said that she had had hysterics twice within the past sixteen hours.

While we waited together, Selena said, 'It's useless, Jennifer. She can't help me. Nobody can. I'm lost, lost.'

'You just talk to her,' I said soothingly. 'That won't hurt anyway. Tell her what happened. See what she says.'

'I don't know what she'll do, what she'll think,' Selena whispered.

I looked around the small room. It was full of bookcases and paintings. The desk was unobtrusive. The curtains were pink, the rug maroon. It was just like someone's study.

I pointed that out to Selena. I said, 'Nothing bad happens here.'

She got to her feet. She took two shaky steps toward the outer door. I'm sure she would have left then, but just at that moment, the nurse came back, said, 'This way, Miss Sellers.'

Selena gave me a single beseeching look before she disappeared into an inner office.

I waited anxiously for her. There was a bustle of movement around me. People came and went, some laughing, some nervously silent. I avoided their eyes just as they avoided mine.

After something less than an hour, Selena returned. Her face was very pale, her eyes red rimmed.

She thrust a paper at me. 'They're sending me home,' she said.

'Home?'

Selena swallowed. 'I told her. It was hard. She listened though. And then...'

'Did she believe you?'

Selena laughed bitterly. 'Oh, come on,

Jennifer. She says I'm having a breakdown, mild version.'

'The scratches?'

'Hysterical stigmata. Marks that come out on the skin, bleed even, from nervous origins, she called them. Like maybe hives, or something.'

A shiver went over me. Dr. Barodini could be right. She was knowledgable, experienced, trained. She *must* be right. But still...

'So I'm to go home for a few weeks and take a rest and see my own doctor and take plenty of phenobarb, and then we'll see.'

'Don't you want to?' I asked. 'Aren't you convinced it will be better?'

'No,' she answered. 'I'm not convinced.'

She stopped on the steps of the Campus Health Center, gave a vague look around.

'I'm sorry, Selena. I guess this is my fault.'

'Yours?'

'If I hadn't made you come here...'

'It doesn't matter, Jennifer. It would have happened one way or another. But I'm not having a breakdown. That's what's really crazy. I'm all right, but nobody will believe me. So I'll have to do what she says.'

Two hours later, Selena was gone. Heartsick, frightened, I told myself that she would be all right soon. She would forget what she had said, her screams and scratches. She would come back and share the room with me again.

59

When I told Dr. Paulen that evening, he nodded, plainly not surprised. He said, 'Yes, that's just exactly what I was afraid of. I saw it coming on, you know.' He shrugged. 'There are still seven of us left.'

Later Jimbill asked me worriedly, 'When's Selena coming back, Jennifer? What's going to happen to her?'

I tried to reassure him, just as I had tried to reassure myself earlier. I said, 'She'll be back in a couple of weeks, Jimbill. You wait and see. It won't take long and she'll be ready for school again.' That time it was I who was so terribly wrong.

Everything was quiet for the next few days. We seven spent our days together, met in class to work on invoking the Group Mind, then returned to the house on Dandy Lane, to pass the evenings in study, talk, and music.

I was aware of a kind of brooding contentment that seemed to have descended on all of us. I saw it in the faces of the others. I felt it in myself. I tried, uneasily, to examine the source of it, but slowly, I forgot to think of it, and merely accepted it as a mood that we all shared as we shared everything else.

I had packed Selena's things, and put them into a closet, ready to be picked up or sent for, but I had no word from her, and when I mentioned it to Dr. Paulen, suggesting that I call her family to find out how she was, he discouraged me.

'I'm quite sure,' he said, 'that it would be better to let her work out this small contretemps of hers by herself. If we make too much of it, she may never recover, you know. She may find it profitable in terms of attention to remain ill.'

I didn't agree with him, but I decided to wait a little longer. I could always get her home address and phone number from the Registrar, I was sure.

But at the end of the same week Selena herself suddenly returned. She walked up Dandy Lane to the house and knocked at the door.

Jimbill was the one who answered it. I heard his delighted welcoming whoop. 'Selena! You're okay! You're home again.'

And I heard her quiet voice, a dull monotone, so strangely unlike her. She said, 'Sure, Jimbill. I'm home.'

I raced into the hallway. She was like a shadow among the shadows. Her blonde hair was dull, unbrushed. Her face was fishbelly white. Her violet eyes were expressionless. I knew then that whatever had troubled her before still troubled her. I knew she wasn't herself.

The next few days proved me right. She had come back to the house, but she had dropped out of school. She moved like a zombie, like a will-less creature, a flesh and bone machine, from room to room. She never spoke unless spoken to first. She never smiled. She never laughed.

Dr. Paulen accepted her return with a shrug. 'If she wants to be here, if it makes her happy, why not?' was all he said.

When I asked her about her parents, she said dully, 'Jennifer, I guess I never explained to you about that. I hate to think about it, or talk about it, but since you asked—'

I cut in, 'Never mind, if you don't want to...'

'There's just one parent really—my Dad. My Mom took off with some beachcomber when I was twelve. I've seen her a couple of times since, but only when she wanted to chisel some money out of my father. Dad's got himself a wife. They have a couple of children. They don't need me or want me. They think I'm trying to get back at them and resent me for it. They know I'm here now. That's all they care about. It doesn't matter what I do.'

'Shouldn't you go to see Dr. Barodini?' I asked.

'There's nothing to go for,' she answered. 'I'm all well now. Can't you see that I'm all well now?'

I knew that she wasn't, but I didn't know what to do about it so I waited—and I waited too long.

*   *   *

62

Abel stood on the gravel road. He looked up at the gray toadlike house and grinned. 'No wonder you finally decided to move here! Why, the atmosphere alone must send your imagination running riot.'

'It's pretty much of a monstrosity, isn't it?' I answered.

His grin faded. He knuckled his short curly hair and frowned, studying me. Finally he said, 'Why are you so itchy?'

'I don't know,' I said first. And then, determined to be honest, I hurried on, 'It's the house partly. A friend of mine had a breakdown here, my roommate really, and that—'

He cut in, frowning still, 'Well, you're not stuck here. Move out. Move back to the dorm.'

I was suddenly aware of Don and Jimbill, sitting on the top step of the porch. I wondered if they could hear any of my conversation with Abel. I said, 'Tell me what you're doing up here.'

'I had to get some material from the dean of the graduate school. I figured that I'd make a day of it and see if I could find you.'

'I'm glad you did, Abel.' That was putting it mildly. I was so glad to see him that my heart was pounding. I didn't dare let him know it.

He leaned closer to me. 'So am I. Look, let's take a ride. Is that all right with you?'

'It's my night to cook,' I said, looking at my watch. 'Will we be back in time for dinner?'

'If you invite me, we will. Otherwise I refuse to guarantee anything.'

'Well ...' I hesitated, not knowing what to say. None of the others had ever brought guests into the house. I didn't know if it was allowed. It might be that there was an unwritten, unspoken rule that forbade strangers. I went on, 'I'll have to find out if it's all right.'

He moved along beside me as I turned toward the house. 'Dr. Paulen's home, so—'

'I want to meet your Dr. Paulen,' Abel interrupted.

Without knowing why, I told him to wait on the porch. 'I'll only be a minute,' I promised.

He gave me a quick sideways look, then nodded. I recognized the sudden look of determination that crossed his face. I went inside quickly.

Dr. Paulen's study was on the top floor, a huge gabled room, that I had seen only once before. I climbed the steps slowly, tapped on his door.

He called, 'Come in, whoever it is.'

I opened the door, stepped inside. He was sitting at his desk, a shadowy silhouette against the bookcases behind him. He smiled, 'And to what do I owe this pleasure, Jennifer?'

'I'd like to have a guest for dinner tonight, Dr. Paulen. Is that all right?'

'Dr. Paulen?' he repeated reproachfully. 'Hank.'

'A guest? Why not? This is your home, isn't it?'

I laughed with relief. I had been almost certain that he would object, though I couldn't for the life of me think why. I backed out of the study hurriedly, tripping on a tangle of wires that lead to a couple of loudspeakers installed on the bookcases. Downstairs I found Abel chatting with Jimbill and Don.

As the two of us walked down to the lane to his car, I told him that Dr. Paulen was glad to have him. I realized, then, that Abel, too, had expected to be refused entrance to the house.

He said, 'That's good because I was going to get in there anyhow.' He paused, then went on in a lowered voice, 'I want to have a good look at your Dr. Paulen, Jennifer. I finally figured out what I'd heard about him. I think you'd better know about it, too.'

I understood at once that he had just given me the reason he had sought me out. It was to talk about Dr. Paulen. My heart began to beat very hard. I felt a blush burn my cheeks. I hurried to the car with Abel, wondering what he would say, suddenly frightened at what he might be about to tell me.

CHAPTER FIVE

Abel drove swiftly down Dandy Lane, the car jolting under us until I protested, 'Why do we have to get so knocked about? If you don't have time to take me for a ride and stay for dinner, all you have to do is say so.'

He gave me a quick glance from clear blue eyes and a wide grin. 'I've got all the time I want.'

'Then stop driving like a madman, and tell me what it is that you know about Dr. Paulen.'

'Do you mind very much if I do it in my own way?'

'I suppose that you will no matter what I say, but you're making me so curious.' I didn't add that he was also making me very nervous, and not just about how he was driving.

'There's something odd about that house, Jennifer,' he said reflectively. 'Or maybe it's not the house. Maybe it's the kids nowadays. When you went inside, I talked to those two guys on the porch.'

'Don Reagon and Jimbill Desiral.'

'They were . . . well, the only way I can put it, I guess, is that they reminded me of a couple of politicians I questioned a few months back— politicians who knew a lot but only wanted to say a little.'

I shrugged. 'Abel, never mind them. What

about Dr. Paulen?'

He asked, 'What do you know about him?'

'Not very much, I suppose. Why?'

'Has he ...' Abel's mouth was narrow around the words, and I saw the muscles move in his jaws with the effort to get them out. 'Has he ever made a pass at you?'

'He has not!' I said indignantly, blushing as I remembered how I yearned toward Dr. Paulen, yet always felt a peculiar fear of him at the same time. I hurried on, 'What's the matter with you anyway? I thought you had something to tell me.'

Abel laughed softly, with relief. 'There's nothing the matter with me. I have a reason for asking.'

'Then suppose you tell me the reason.' Again I felt my heart begin to beat faster. What was Abel driving at? What had he learned?

'Has he ever made passes at the other girls in the house?' Abel asked soberly. 'Don't jump at me, and don't answer before you think. Has he, that you know of?'

'Of course not,' I retorted. Then I thought of Selena. Had Dr. Paulen ever given any sign that he was interested in her? I tried to think back. It was hard to remember. The past two months seemed blurred in my mind, but I thought, I was almost certain, that he had treated Selena, me, the other girls, all alike. That he had treated us just as he treated the boys. And as for making passes—no. No, I was almost certain. Nothing like that could have happened. I would have noticed. I would have heard something.

'All right. That's to the good then,' Abel was saying, 'because you see, what I finally remembered about him has to do with that.'

'I don't know what you mean.'

'He taught at a university in California until last year,' Abel explained. 'He left under a cloud of some sort. I don't know just what. But I think it had to do with his dating some of his girl students—and carrying matters somewhat further than respectability allows for.'

I knew that some people would think that was the worst thing in the world, but I found that I couldn't get very excited about it. Dr. Paulen wasn't an old man, and he was alone, and . . . then I remembered. He had had a son, a wife. I didn't know what had happened to them. I supposed there was a divorce. Anyway, he was alone now. If a girl appealed to him—I pulled my thoughts up short. I had just told Abel that Dr. Paulen had not shown any interest in the girls in the seminar. Then why was I considering the morality of it?

'You realize why I brought this up, don't you, Jennifer?'

I shook my head.

'It's because you moved into the house. I never did get the straight of it. How come you left the dorm? How come the whole class, all eight of you, shifted over to Dandy Lane?'

I hardly knew the answer to that myself. I said, 'Well, Jimbill said it was rent free, so he jumped at it, and Mike, too. He's on a football scholarship, and so he—'

'Why do you suppose Dr. Paulen offered everybody free lodgings?'

'I guess he was lonesome. It's a big place, and—' I stopped because I had finally seen what Abel was driving at. 'Oh, you think he had us all move in so he could seduce the girls. Is that it?'

'There's the possibility.'

'No. I'm sure it's not that. It's something else.' But what else? I asked myself. Why had he been so willing to give up his privacy, to share his home with all of us?

'I don't like playing the role of a man passing on rumors—especially rumors that might be completely unfounded—but I'd just as soon that you watch out for him, Jennifer.'

'You don't have to worry about me,' I said stiffly.

'Don't I?'

'No. I'm certain. He's never ... he wouldn't ever ...'

Abel nodded. 'Okay. I accept that. But the last time you were home, last month, wasn't it, you spoke about the seminar to me.'

'Yes. I remember. Your mother fed me milk and cookies and you told me that I had a good imagination, and that I was bored and looking for an excuse to drop out of the seminar and of school.' I twisted my hands in my lap and looked straight ahead. I wished suddenly that Abel hadn't come to the house, that I hadn't gone for a ride with him.

He laughed. 'You sound so bitter, Jennifer. I'm sorry about that. I apologize. And I want to tell you that I kept on thinking about how you felt, and finally I decided to find out what I could about Dr. Paulen. You've always been a level-headed kid, in spite of that imagination of yours, and I ought to know, oughtn't I? So I couldn't be satisfied with the explanation I gave you and myself. That's why I first checked Dr. Paulen out, and that's why I'm going to keep checking him out.'

I moved restlessly. I said, 'It didn't have anything to do with him.'

'I know you spoke about the course, Jennifer, but I felt that somehow, intuitively, maybe, you might have sensed something wrong.'

That was when I should have told him more about Selena and her breakdown. I have no excuse for not doing that. I have no explanation. I just didn't want to talk about her. I didn't want to try to put my fear into words. I think I was afraid that he would call me a silly kid and laugh at me, or maybe I was afraid that he would give me away, say something before the others, or ask too pointed a question. Anyhow, I let the moment pass.

'It had nothing to do with Dr. Paulen,' I repeated.

'What about the course? Is it interesting now?'

'Yes.'

'Does it still give you the willies?'

I couldn't lie to him. I said, evading the truth, 'I guess it's just me, Abel. Nobody else seems—' But I stopped myself. That last would have been a lie. I knew perfectly well how much everyone in the seminar had changed since the course began.

'Yes?'

I shrugged, repeated, 'I guess it's just me.'

'Then you're not going to drop it?'

'I don't think so.'

'I gather that you're not as bored as you were. Is that it?'

'I suppose it is,' I agreed.

Abel knuckled his dark hair, then glanced at me. 'Okay. But take the word of an old man, will you, Jennifer? Just keep your eye on Dr. Paulen. Make sure he doesn't decide that you're the prettiest girl around—which you are, of course—but I'd just as soon he didn't notice.'

'He hasn't, and he won't,' I grinned. 'If he notices anybody it'll be Harriet Varnum, who is a real sexpot, only a little dumb for him, or maybe Bess Ardway, who is another one, but very smart.'

'These I have to see,' Abel laughed.

71

I didn't answer him. I remembered the strange glances we exchanged the first time I saw Dr. Paulen in class. I wondered if that had been based on a mild flirtatiousness in him, and then I realized that I wished he had paid more attention to me than he actually had. I was always glad of the very rare few moments we had alone together. I didn't mention that to Abel. I didn't see that he had to know about it. It would only provoke further warnings from him.

He glanced at his watch. 'I guess it's time to go back to the haunted house.'

'Haunted house,' I echoed. 'Why do you say that?'

Abel frowned. 'You sound so shaken. When did you get to be afraid of ghosts?'

'I'm not. It's just...'

'I called it a haunted house because it's a great old ugly place and should have been torn down years ago and to tell you the truth, I can't for the life of me see why you'd rather live there than in a new clean beautiful dorm.'

'We're all together there, you see,' I explained.

'You could all be together some place else just as well,' Abel retorted. 'And being together could be too much of a good thing anyway.'

I didn't answer him.

'Who else do you see—besides that group, I mean? What else do you do?'

'Things,' I said vaguely.

72

He didn't press me further. He was silent as he drove me back to the house, parked in the lane.

As we went up the road together, I shivered. I felt the same apprehension mixed with anticipation that I always felt on entering the house.

Harriet met us in the foyer. 'I've set the table for you,' she said, dimpling at Abel, plainly waiting for the introduction she expected me to make.

I obliged her as politely as I could, asked her to entertain Abel and introduce him to the others as they came in, and then hurried into the kitchen.

I was sure that Harriet was Abel's type, and that they would get along just fine. There was equally no doubt in my mind that Harriet would like him. I grumpily wished them all joy in each other, and then wished I'd never asked Abel to stay for dinner.

I had just turned the flame on under the stew when Dr. Paulen came in. 'Is your guest here?' he asked, his gleaming eyes narrowed.

I nodded, busily mixing salad.

'I suppose he's a friend of yours from your hometown.'

'A neighbor,' I explained. 'He lives down the street from me.'

'Oh. Then you've known him a long time.'

'Just about all my life,' I agreed.

I told myself that it was natural for Dr.

73

Paulen to be curious about Abel. But I wished he would stop asking questions. He wasn't through, however.

There was a teasing inflection in his voice when he went on, 'I expect he got so lonesome for you that he just had to come up and see you.'

I glanced up.

Dr. Paulen's dark eyes seemed full of points of golden light, as if the gold emblem on his rolled collar was reflected in the wet coal depths of his eyes.

I said, 'Abel's a newspaperman. He's up here on a story, so he stopped to say hello.'

'Then he's not really your boyfriend?'

Remembering what Abel had been saying earlier, I felt a blush burn my cheeks. Why was Dr. Paulen asking me such things? If Abel heard him, he would surely think that Dr. Paulen was showing just that interest in me that Abel had warned me against.

Aloud I said, 'No, he's not my boyfriend.'

I heard Harriet giggle, and thought crossly that it was my luck to have kitchen duty tonight, just when Abel was here. I heard Abel's deep laughter, and decided that next time he happened by the campus I would just be too busy to see him.

Dr. Paulen sat at the work table, idly tasting the salad dressing. 'Needs more garlic, I think. Would you get it, Jennifer?'

I went into the pantry, looked on the lower

shelf. I didn't see the garlic there so I checked the other shelves. I found it on the top one. It was just like Harriet to decide to put things where she could reach them, being tall, instead of remembering that I had a real struggle to reach the top shelf.

I brought the garlic back to Dr. Paulen, and he thanked me absently. He crushed some into the salad dressing, gave it a good shake, murmured, 'There that should be fine.'

Soon after, he left me alone. I sliced bread, put out butter, rechecked the table. Then, as soon as the stew was hot, I rang the bell. The others came in, settled at the table. Harriet lit the candles. Bess started the casseroles around.

Dr. Paulen smiled faintly at Abel. 'I understand you're a newspaperman.'

Abel looked startled. 'Oh? How did you know that?'

'In the first place, you have that bright curious intent look that most reporters have. In the second, Jennifer told me,' Dr. Paulen answered.

We all laughed.

Dr. Paulen went on, 'It isn't a secret, is it?'

'No, certainly not.'

'You're here on business, I suppose,' Dr. Paulen went on.

'Yes, I am. There's been talk in the state capital of new departments being developed in the graduate school. I had to see the dean to find out what he's planning, if anything.'

'Interesting. I hadn't heard anything about that.'

'It's very nebulous, I find now.' Abel looked around the table. 'I understand that this is one of your classes. Right here and now. That's a very unusual situation, isn't it?'

'Unusual?' Dr. Paulen asked.

'For a class to study together and live together, too, I mean.'

Dr. Paulen's dark eyes narrowed. 'It is perfectly in order,' he answered.

'Of course,' Abel said hastily. 'I wasn't implying anything else. I just meant that not many professors are willing to be on the job twenty-four hours a day every day. Most want times with their families. Most want some privacy.'

'This is my family,' Dr. Paulen said stiffly.

I stopped staring at the gold-framed paintings on the wall, the child's paintings of tilted trees and falling-down houses, and a three-legged bear.

I looked at Abel. He gave a quizzical smile, then asked, 'Your course, Dr. Paulen, the Group Mind ... it sounds very interesting to me.'

'Oh? Has Jennifer discussed that with you?'

'Just a little. But that little has made me very curious.'

'Newspapermen are by nature curious, aren't they?' Dr. Paulen said. And then he said nothing else.

There was sudden heavy silence. The candlelight flickered as if a draft had blown through the window. Shadows danced on the walls. I saw Don and Jimbill exchange glances. I saw Harriet's hands freeze on the table and Bess's fingers turn white around the fork she held. I saw Selena shrink back in her chair.

Mike and Victor both started to speak at the same time. Mike's gravelly voice overrode Victor's stutter. But then they both stopped. The heavy silence returned.

At last Dr. Paulen said, 'The concept is interesting, of course, but so far we've done little with it.'

'No results? Is that what you mean?' Abel asked, in a voice that told me he was very nearly teasing.

Dr. Paulen didn't seem to realize that. He answered gravely, 'We've only been at it since September. It will take many months, many months more, before we can say whether we've learned anything important. We have a long way to go and after that it may take many months before we can prove it—If there's anything to prove, of course.'

Harriet opened her mouth, and Bess nudged her.

Mike said, 'It's fun anyhow,' and squinted at the candle flame.

'I imagine it is,' Abel agreed. 'I'd like to know how you go about devising experiments.'

Dr. Paulen passed the casserole again, and

everyone helped himself, and by the time that flurry of motion was over, Dr. Paulen was talking about a summer vacation he'd had in the Yucatan.

Soon after, with dinner finished, Abel apologized for having to go. I was regretful but relieved. I had felt all the time he was in the house that I was walking on eggshells. That the others were. I sensed that Dr. Paulen was disturbed by Abel's questions. I couldn't see why, and not seeing why troubled me.

I went out to the car with Abel. He bent, lightly kissed me good night. He said, 'Be a good girl, Jennifer, and study hard.'

I remembered how he and Harriet had laughed together while I worked in the kitchen. I remembered how her eyes had gone back to him again and again at the table, and it seemed to me that he had been showing off in his questions to Dr. Paulen, showing off for her. I knew how I would feel when he was gone. Deserted, defenseless, with Abel gone. It was just too much.

I snapped, 'Abel Harding, I am not ten years old any more. I'd appreciate it if you tried to remember that.'

'Hey,' he said, surprised but sober, 'what's all this?'

I amazed myself by bursting into tears. 'I don't know,' I sobbed. 'You just make me so mad.'

He held me against him for a moment. Then

he gave me a small shake and moved away from me. 'You really are strung tight, aren't you? You, and everybody in that house. I could feel it. I know it. Don't you want to tell me what's bothering you?'

'Nothing. You've been here. You've seen for yourself. Now you know. Nothing's bothering me.'

'Something about the seminar,' he said thoughtfully. He caught me by the shoulders. 'All right, Jennifer. I refused to take you seriously the last time you brought it up. I'm sorry. I was wrong. I apologize. Does that mean that you're never going to trust me again? No matter what?'

I looked up at him, and tried to think of the words. I hesitated for a moment, and that brief time was too long.

The door opened. Dr. Paulen stood in an oblong of pale yellow light, and then, lighting his pipe as he came, he joined us on the gravel road.

'Beautiful evening, isn't it?' he said, though there were thick clouds in the sky, and the chill wet wind seemed to cut through my heavy jacket. 'Beautiful evening,' he repeated.

Somehow he started us moving. We were suddenly at Abel's car, and he was with us.

Abel gave me a helpless look, then grinned. 'Take care of yourself, Jennifer. I'll see you soon. Very soon.' And to Dr. Paulen, 'Thanks for your hospitality. It was all very interesting.'

79

Within moments, he was gone.

I was alone again in the house on Dandy Lane.

Dr. Paulen said, 'I like your friend. He's a clever man, isn't he?' in a voice that told me he didn't like Abel at all.

I said only, 'I think he's clever.'

'So do I, Jennifer. So do I,' Dr. Paulen laughed.

It seemed to me that I heard that same soft knowing laughter at the beginning of the dream. It bubbled and echoed around me, familiar and warm, but somehow frightening, too. I wanted to wake up but I couldn't. I heard the laughter and remembered how still Selena had been when I'd come into the room. That stillness had frightened me and I had stood over her. Her body hardly showed under the sheet. She had become that thin. Her slenderness was emaciation. I had found myself breathing easier when I saw her small shallow breaths. At last, turning away, on edge and worried, I had gone to bed.

Sometime thereafter, when the clouds broke for a moment and spilled moonlight into the room, I awakened briefly. I looked at Selena. She was motionless. I turned over and fell asleep again.

The soft knowing laughter began again. It enveloped me and echoed through me. I fought it, trying to wake myself up, but I found myself drowning in it, in soft knowing laughter.

Then, suddenly, it was gone. A thick heavy dark cloud floated over my bed. It was evil, foul smelling. It dripped noxious fluids upon me, and stroked me with clammy tentacles. It nudged me delicately, and left burning pain behind. It teased and tormented and terrified me, and I lay there, staring up at it, conscious but still asleep. I watched it and knew what it was. I was trapped in the dream and I couldn't escape. I was afraid that I would never escape. I would die in that dream and never see daylight, never see Abel...

I came out of it slowly. I thought I was still sleeping, still dreaming, when I pulled myself to the edge of the bed and forced myself into a sitting position.

Selena was sitting on the floor on the oval rug. Her violet eyes were big, blind with terror. She asked in a hoarse whisper, 'Jennifer, what's the matter with you? What happened during the night?'

CHAPTER SIX

What happened during the night? I wondered. I huddled on the edge of the bed, quivering. I could still hear the soft knowing laughter. I could still see the black cloud that had hung over me, and feel its terrible touch, and smell its foul odor. I was weak, bloodless, as if while I

81

slept a vampire had sucked from my body every vital fluid, all strength and power.

I met Selena's glance only briefly, fearful that she would see in my eyes the horror that filled me. I drew a deep steadying breath. Then I said, as coolly as I could, 'I guess I had a nightmare. Why are you asking what happened?'

'You moaned,' she said hoarsely. 'You moaned, Jennifer, and cried, and begged. You pleaded with me to wake you up, and when I tried you fought me savagely, as if you thought I was your attacker.'

'I fought you?' I tried to smile. 'I'm sorry, Selena. I didn't mean it, of course. I didn't know—'

'That doesn't matter.' She turned her head and I saw the healing marks on her throat. The dim light fell on her face and I saw the dark circles under her dull eyes. She went on, 'I've been watching you for hours, Jennifer. There's no use in your pretending, not with me. I've been there. I've experienced it. I know. It visited me first, and now it's visited you. The Group Mind. I know. I know. Why don't you admit the truth?'

But Selena was sick, I told myself quickly. She'd had a breakdown. Dr. Barodini had said so. Selena had had a breakdown and either scratched herself with the nailfile I'd found in the corner, or else her own sickness had torn her skin from within in some way I didn't

82

understand. I couldn't believe anything she told me. I mustn't. And most of all, I didn't dare allow her to influence me. Maybe even now, without my realizing it, my dreams had been infected by her weird delusions. Within me there was a whispered question: Are they delusions? I didn't listen. I didn't answer.

I said firmly, 'I just had a silly dream, Selena.'

In those words I heard a strange echo of what Selena herself had insisted so often to me. I realized now how sometimes she spoke of the Group Mind, and at other times she denied it, claimed she had dreamed it all. Was I, at this moment, trying to do what she had done? Was I trying to hide from my fear lest it engulf me entirely? What if I admitted to Selena what had happened? Would that be confirmation of her illness? Would she worsen? Then, would she, in trying to prove her own sanity, tell the others about me? Would they think me mad as they now thought poor Selena mad? As I did myself?

A shiver touched me. I jumped to my feet. I said, 'Selena, don't you think you ought to go home? What's the use of hanging around here doing nothing? If you aren't in school, then ...'

She gave me a long silent look. She brushed her tangled blonde hair from her thin cheeks. She stood up shakily, and went to her bed and stretched out on it, closing her eyes.

'It's not that I don't want you, you know,' I

said hastily. 'It's for your own good.'

She kept her eyes closed and whispered, 'Jennifer, don't. I explained about my Dad, about his wife. I don't belong there with them, and besides . . . I can't go. I have to stay here.'

'But why?' I demanded. 'It's no good for you being alone in the house all day doing nothing and not seeing anybody but us. It's not—' I stopped. There was Jimbill. Maybe she felt she had to stay because of him, to cling to him. I said, 'You'd keep in contact with us, you know. Jimbill and I, we'd come to see you.'

She didn't answer me. She rolled over and buried her face in her folded arms.

*   *   *

I began to dread the nights, knowing that the moment I fell asleep the amorphous cloud would gather over my bed, knowing that I would feel its evil drip on me, stroke me, sting me. I wished that I dared admit it, but Selena's pale haunted face kept me silent, reminded me through long frightening days that if I spoke to anyone, anyway at all, I might be resigning myself to her fate. The words, once said, might break my hold on reality. I didn't dare take the chance. At the same time, I worried about Selena. I knew that something had to be done to save her. I knew a threat hung over her.

One gray morning, when Dr. Paulen was sitting at the kitchen table, watching as I

84

prepared breakfast, I said, 'Selena looks so terrible. Don't you think her father should know?'

'Perhaps. But I believe it would be very unkind to send her away,' he answered.

'But if she doesn't have help, treatment...'

His black eyes narrowed over his beard. 'What if there's no help, Jennifer?'

'There has to be,' I protested. 'Dr. Barodini said she...'

He sat very still. When he answered me his voice had that strange timbre that often touched me with cold. He asked, 'Do you really believe that there's help for everyone, a solution to all problems, an anodyne for all pain, all terror, all human tragedy?'

'I don't know about all—but for Selena ... yes, yes, there must be a way!'

He smiled faintly, 'Then why don't you go to speak with Dr. Barodini? Tell her that Selena has returned, and explain how she is now. Perhaps Dr. Barodini would—' He stopped himself. 'I don't want you to misunderstand me. I'm not telling you to do this, to involve yourself.'

'I am involved,' I retorted. 'She's my friend.'

He smiled again. 'What you do is up to you, of course.' He got to his feet. 'Take the toast in, Jennifer. I'll bring the coffee.'

I did as he told me, and moments later he followed me into the dining room. He set the coffee pot on the table, then switched on the overhead light. The blues and greens of the shade seemed to gather in his face. I suddenly saw him as a saint in a stained-glass window, a saint who lived only partly in this world.

He said, 'You're a good girl, Jennifer. You're the strong one, aren't you?'

I felt my cheeks flush with pleasure at his praise. I knew how I had come to enjoy the few moments we had alone together. The quick exchanges we had time for when he came into the kitchen before meals. He always did that. I briefly wondered why, then dismissed it, thinking that always, in the presence of the others, he maintained the same bantering relationship with me that he did with them. When we two were alone, it was like the first time I had seen him. I sensed an unspoken exchange between us. I felt something draw me closer and closer to him, as if he knew all the secrets of my heart and mind, knew even those secrets I still concealed from myself but would some day learn.

Then I remembered Abel. The flush in my cheeks became a sting of embarassment. Abel would say I was exhibiting all the symptoms of a school-girl crush on an older man. He would laugh, tousle my hair, tease me as if I were a kid. I knew it wasn't a crush. Mixed with this odd sense of closeness, of joy at Dr. Paulen's small recognitions, there was something else. Some small core within me withdrew in uneasy self-protection. I was wary of him. I couldn't, without being reminded, call him by his first name.

He went on, 'Yes. You're the strong one. So you're the logical one to worry about Selena, to do something for her. The others ...' He shrugged, and didn't finish.

In the sweetness of the look he gave me, I forgot about my terrible dream-filled nights. I forgot about Abel. I gave up my reservations. I determined that I would help Selena no matter what it took. I knew Dr. Paulen was right. I was the only one who could. The others all seemed strangely detached, wrapped in the cocoons of their own concerns. They gave only brief attention to Selena. That was what Dr. Paulen had left unsaid.

That afternoon, after my English class, I went to the Campus Health Center to see Dr. Barodini. I had to wait for an hour and a half, under the stare of the nurse. When, at last, I was ushered in to see the psychiatrist, she listened to me disapprovingly. I told her that Selena had returned to stay at the house. I explained what she looked like, how she acted.

'I can not treat her through an intermediary,' Dr. Barodini said, toying with the pearls that hung at her throat. 'You must bring her to see me.'

'She won't come. I've asked her several times, really tried to persuade her, and she won't come.'

'How is she doing in her courses?'

I realized only then that I hadn't explained that Selena had actually dropped out of school. I told Dr. Barodini.

She frowned, 'Don't you realize that if she's not in school, not a student, that I can do nothing for her?'

'She's terribly sick,' I insisted. 'You saw how she was before. You called it a breakdown.'

'There are twenty thousand students at the university. Do you realize what a case load I already have? I can't handle even one that doesn't belong here.'

I stared at her, hardly believing my ears. Selena was sick. The woman before me was a doctor. She was refusing to help. I couldn't accept that.

I whispered, 'Don't you understand what I'm trying to tell you? She's a lot worse now than she was. Suppose it goes on. Suppose something happens?'

'I'm sorry,' Dr. Barodini retorted.

'Then what should I do?' I asked.

'Send her home.'

'I can't. She won't go.'

'Isn't your housemother aware?'

I realized then that Selena hadn't explained that she didn't live in the dorm. I told Dr. Barodini about the house, about Dr. Paulen. I told her that when I had spoken to him, he had said it would be cruel to force Selena to leave.

She hardly listened to me, I could tell. When I paused, she said, 'It's his house, then it's his responsibility.'

'But it's ours! Yours and mine, too!'

She gave me a level look, then reached for her appointment pad. 'I have a patient waiting,' she told me.

I left her without a word.

I knew I ought to go to the library to work on my midterm paper for philosophy. Instead I went back to the house on Dandy Lane.

The boulevard had been crowded with laughing groups making plans for the three-day Thanksgiving recess. I had been toying with the idea of going home, but I finally put it aside. I didn't know why exactly. It would have been a relief to be away even for a few days, to sleep in my own bed at home with my parents down the hall, and Abel down the street. Surely I would forget my terrible dreams in that most familiar of atmospheres. Still, without quite knowing why, I decided I wouldn't go home.

As I turned into the lane, I left the laughing young people behind me. Here all was silence, and emptiness. The bare limbs of the bushes arched overhead, forming a skeletal tunnel through which twilight shown in splinters of gray. The tall stone posts loomed up, casting straight black shadows on the wallow of dried leaves.

Another shadow stood there, a third. It was as unmoving as the ones cast by the stone pillars. Alarm touched me, spilled heat through my chilled flesh, quickened my pulses.

I paused.

The shadow turned and became Don. He said, 'That you, Jennifer?'

I nodded. 'Of course it's me. Why are you standing here in the cold?'

He shrugged his lanky body. His hazel eyes skidded away from my searching glance.

'Don't you want to go in?' I asked.

'I don't know.' Now he stared at me intently. 'Sometimes I do, and sometimes I don't. Do you understand what I mean?'

I thought of the strange mixture of attraction and repulsion that swept me every time I entered the house. Yes. I knew what he meant, but dared I admit it to him? Would he suddenly laugh at me? Would he tell the others. Would I become the same object of pity and contempt that poor Selena was now?

He said slowly, 'I guess you think I'm nuts, don't you?'

'No. No, I don't, Don.'

'It's ... well, you have to admit it, it's pretty eerie. I guess it's just my imagination.'

'What is?'

I saw that we were circling each other, feeling each other out, trying to speak without quite speaking directly. Both of us were fearful of giving ourselves away. I wondered, suddenly, if Don, too, was plagued in the silence of the nights by a whispering amorphous cloud. I didn't dare ask him. I was afraid of what he might tell me.

He was saying, 'Everything's eerie. The way Selena is, the things she says and then denies. Haven't you noticed? There's the rest of us, too. I mean, are we the same as we were? Do you think so?'

'I ...' I hesitated, not knowing what to answer, how much to admit, how far I could trust him.

'You're not the same, Jennifer.'

'Of course I am,' I said quickly.

'No.'

'But why not? How do you mean?'

He shrugged again. 'How do I know why not?'

I was suddenly frightened. I didn't understand why, but I felt small quick explosions of fear prick my skin. I looked up at the house. There was a face, a pale blur of a face, at the window of Dr. Paulen's top floor study.

Don asked, 'What's the matter?'

'Nothing.' I started up the gravel road, and he fell into step beside me. 'Are you going home for Thanksgiving?' I asked, hoping the question would divert him from what he had been saying to me.

He answered, 'No, I guess not. Though I expect my father's going to be plenty sore.'

'Sore?'

'He got tickets for the Army-Navy game. It took plenty of wire-pulling, I'll bet.'

'Then why don't you go, Don? Mike would

give anything to be in your shoes.'

Don grinned faintly. 'Mike would, but I wouldn't. I don't know. I just don't feel like it, and besides, my father's a real hard-core Establishment type. He'll take one look at my hair hanging down my shoulders, and start swearing, and end up dragging me to a barber.'

I was reminded then that Don's father was Jared Reagon, the criminal lawyer, a man Abel had spoken of often with admiration and respect. I didn't mention that to Don. Judging by the way he spoke, he wouldn't want me to.

Instead, I grinned, 'In that case, maybe it is better that you stay here. I don't think I'd know you with a brush cut.'

'I wouldn't know myself.'

'I'm staying, too,' I said.

'You are? How come?'

I couldn't tell if he was pleased or just surprised. I answered, 'Well, there's a midterm paper I've got to get done, and . . . well, I don't know. I just thought . . .'

'You just don't want to leave either,' he said firmly. 'That's really what it is, isn't it?'

'Don't want to?' I protested. 'Oh, sure. Sure I do. But I think, really, maybe I'd better not. I mean, the paper and I have other things to do.'

'All excuses,' he told me, smiling faintly. 'You're doing what I'm doing, what all of us are doing, just making up excuses so we don't have to leave.'

We had reached the house by then. I forced

92

myself up the steps to the porch. I forced myself to reach for the doorknob. At the same time, Don reached for it, too. Our fingers met. I pulled mine away quickly.

He said softly, 'Nobody's going home. Doesn't that seem funny to you? That none of us are going home for Thanksgiving?'

I didn't answer him. I couldn't. He had opened the door, and warm dark air rushed out to engulf me. I lost my breath in it and my lungs couldn't function. For a moment it was like the dream come true. The amorphous cloud, dark and heavy, smelling putrid and burning, settled over me. Was Don right? Was it odd that we had all elected to stay in the house? Were we all fearful of leaving it? Did we, unknown to each other, share the same secret terrors?

Don asked, 'What's the matter, Jennifer? Can't you see?'

I was freed then. I breathed deeply of the cold outside air, shook myself, and went inside.

I made myself walk up the steps, glad that Don went with me. He turned off into his room.

I heard him say, just as the door closed, 'Hey, Vic, what are you doing?'

I moved slowly, unwillingly, down the long dark hall. Passing Harriet's room, I paused. I wondered if Don had been right. Were we really all staying here? I could believe it of the rest of us, but Harriet was different. She spoke so often of her home and family. I knew her burden of loneliness. I could hardly believe that she wouldn't seize the chance, the excuse, to see everybody. I decided to ask her why she was letting the opportunity pass by, or at least to find out if Don was right that she intended to.

I tapped at the door.

There was no answer, but I heard the sound of movement inside. I thought I heard a subdued sniff.

I tapped again, louder.

Harriet said, 'What?' in a hoarse shaky voice.

'It's me. Jennifer.'

'Don't come in,' she cried.

Something in her hoarse voice, in the very words, made me throw the door open.

She was sitting at a table before the window. Her haggard face was wet with tears. Her high cheek bones were too sharp, her big smoky eyes dull. She sobbed. 'What's wrong with you? Are you deaf or something? I said don't come in, and I meant it. Go away, Jennifer.'

I closed the door gently. I asked, 'All right. I'll go away in a minute, but what's happened. What's wrong?'

I felt my pulses quickening. I felt fresh stirrings of alarm begin in my chest.

'Nothing's happened. Nothing's wrong,' she wailed. 'Just leave me alone.'

'What's the matter?' I insisted.

'I want to go home,' she moaned. 'Oh, I want

to so bad. I want to see my sister and brother and help Mother cook the turkey.'

'Then why don't you? You've got three days off. There's no reason why you can't get on a bus and—'

'I just can't.'

'Why?'

She took a deep shaky breath. 'I guess I'm scared, that's why. I don't dare go. I don't dare see them.'

I stared at her.

Fresh tears welled in her eyes, and she folded over the table like a punctured balloon. 'Don't ask me why,' she said in a hoarse broken voice, 'because I don't know why.'

I pulled up a chair, sat beside her. I took her hand. I said, 'Harriet, you're all upset over nothing. If you want to go home so much, then go. You don't have to be scared of your folks. I can tell by everything that you say about them that you get along just great.'

'It's not them, Jennifer. It's me. I'm afraid of what I'll say.'

'Afraid of what you'll say?' I echoed. 'But, Harriet...'

It was then that she told me. Sweet, giggly, not very bright Harriet, who was here on the boy bit and had a terrible time studying because she didn't care about school. All she cared about was getting married and setting up a home and family just like the one she came from.

She whispered, 'The things in my mind, Jennifer. The terrible nights. The awful whispers I hear. I'm sick. I know it. I'm just like Selena, but worse, worse! I don't dare tell them. They'll never put up with it. They'll lock me away, and I'll be sick with shame that I couldn't make school. I can't. I can't because of the awful things in my mind. I can't even trust myself anymore because of those awful things in my mind.'

I went over the list in my head. Selena screaming in agony. I myself awakening each morning to find my pillow damp with the cold sweat of terror. Now Harriet...

I squeezed Harriet's hand as hard as I could, trying to impart to her a strength I didn't feel and knew I didn't have. I sat there, silent as the stone posts outside, my throat clogged with fear.

What had happened to the three of us? What more would happen?

CHAPTER SEVEN

It was after Thanksgiving dinner.

We had all worked on it together, pooling our talents. Harriet had stuffed the turkey, using a recipe her mother had given her and insisted that all of us, Selena included, must watch while she did it.

Selena had contributed cranberry and orange relish. I had made candied sweet potatoes. Mike and Don had done the salad and Jimbill had concocted a famous New Orleans dressing. Victor and Bess had covered themselves with flour, and glory, too, baking pumpkin pies from a cookbook they'd bought at the campus store. Dr. Paulen had been the overseer, making quick grinning suggestions, and trading quips while the rest of us worried over the possible success or failure of our labors.

There had been no failures, and the day had been the best I remembered in the house. It was as if no shadow hung over Selena and Harriet, none over me, or the others. I felt as if we had all submerged ourselves in the joyous holiday, escaping from evil memories. We were all whole that day, safe, and happy.

The only dissatisfaction I had—and it was mine alone—was that I hadn't had a minute by myself with Dr. Paulen. We had milled around in the kitchen together. We had tripped over each other in the dining room. The eight of us were a single unit, a single body. I had waited hopefully, through the hours, for some special smile or word from him, but none came. I found myself wishing the day would end so that I could look forward to the next one. Perhaps then...

But now we were gathered in the living room. Dr. Paulen brought out a bottle of wine, and suggested a fire. Don and Mike went to work. Soon the beautiful flames leaped on the grate, threw flickering shadows on the walls.

Bess played the guitar, her husky voice filling the room with old Scottish ballads and mournful mountain songs. Her auburn hair seemed to sparkle with embers, and her deep brown eyes seemed to sparkle with unshed tears.

Selena sat in a corner of the sofa, her face a pale shadow. Jimbill, as always, was beside her, leaning back. Below, Harriet and Mike sat shoulder to shoulder on cushions before the fireplace. Her long blonde hair fell in a sheaf across his tanned, very muscular arm.

Redheaded Victor sat in one easy chair, his green eyes gleaming beneath short stubby lashes. I sat in the other one. Don was stretched out at my feet, watching the flame silhouettes on the ceiling. Dr. Paulen leaned at the mantel, his lips moving within his dark beard, his head bent, as if listening to the words of Bess's songs, and singing them along with her.

It was peaceful, quiet. I favored that moment then. I savor it in memory still. I wanted it to go on forever. I wish now that it had. We were all then, in those moments, ourselves. Our souls and hearts were at peace. We didn't know what was to come. I didn't ask myself what went on behind those quiet faces. I didn't wonder what shadows darkened within. I didn't search beyond the facades for answers.

I accepted those moments as what they appeared to be, as what I wanted to be, I see now. We were at peace.

Then Don sat up, wrapped his arms around his legs, as if bracing himself. He looked at Dr. Paulen. 'What do you think will come of it?' he asked, his hazel eyes intent, direct, demanding.

Dr. Paulen turned his head slowly. 'What?'

'What do you think will come of it, Dr. Paulen?'

I realized then that Don had as much trouble accustoming himself to use the professor's first name as I did.

Dr. Paulen raised his dark brows.

Don grinned. 'Okay. What do you think will come of it, Hank?'

I felt a strange stir in the room. The flames leaped high suddenly, then fell, as the logs in the grate collapsed to gleaming embers. The room darkened perceptibly.

Don went on not waiting for Dr. Paulen to comment, 'Of our seminar, I mean.'

'We'll go on,' Dr. Paulen answered. 'We've made an interesting start, wouldn't you say?'

'Go on to what?' Don asked.

I was reminded then that his father was a lawyer. I wondered if Don would go into law. I thought perhaps not. Then I thought that maybe he would but didn't yet know that himself.

'We'll go on to more experiments,' Dr. Paulen answered, 'and to greater knowledge.

That's what our goal is, greater knowledge.'

'Can we do it?' Don asked.

Dr. Paulen filled Don's glass first, then Harriet's, then Victor's. After that he filled the others. Then he said, 'That remains to be seen, Don, but what we're learning is invaluable.'

'Invaluable?' Don repeated in a questioning voice. 'Invaluable? I don't know. I don't see it.'

I wished that Don hadn't interrupted the sweet silence. I wished with all my heart that he had allowed our peaceful evening to continue. I wished he had let us drink our wine, listen to Bess sing.

'If the seminar is of no use to you—' Dr. Paulen began.

But Don cut in, 'I didn't say that at all. It's just ... well, I don't know how to explain it exactly, but I've been thinking about our concepts, thinking hard, Dr. Paulen, these past couple of months.'

'And?' Dr. Paulen's voice was silky, smooth, but I heard the familiar undercurrent in it. A shiver went up my back. I wanted Don to stop talking. It was Thanksgiving. A holiday. We were out of class for three days. We were on vacation. Why did he have to spoil our fun with his questions now?

I gave him a resentful look, but he either didn't see it, or else he just ignored it.

He said, 'I think we've gone off the track. We've forgotten that we're trying to study mob psychology.'

'And how is that?' Dr. Paulen asked interestedly.

'The Group Mind,' Don said. 'You can explain mob psychology without getting so far afield, I think.'

'Oh, can you?'

'I think so,' Don said stubbornly. 'The whole idea verges too closely on the supernatural. It...'

'Perhaps,' Dr. Paulen began, 'and perhaps not. It depends on how you look at it, of course. Many men think of the human mind as being supernatural. Philosophy and religion both are attempts to deal with that quality of man. As for me, I rather think that it is not a supernatural attitude at all. I believe our concept will lead us to understand the minds of men in groups. But that does remain to be seen. What I think is not important. The scientific method requires a study of every possibility. The possibility of the Group Mind, existing, as if born by the union of many minds, is a new one. You'll notice, Don, that I've just used the wording of an analogy you suggested long ago in the seminar. The analogy of a child produced by the union of a man and a woman, a child which then becomes separate from the both of them.'

If Don was pleased, or even heard that reference, he gave no sign. He tugged his shoulder length sandy hair, and peered into Dr. Paulen's face.

Dr. Paulen went on, almost in a whisper, 'We are merely trying to test that new concept.'

There was a sudden restiveness in the room. Bess had been holding her guitar, fingers ready, as if she would soon play again, but now she set the guitar aside. Jimbill took Selena's lace-thin hand in his, and hitched closer to her. Harriet took a loud gasping breath. Mike emptied his wine glass and put it down and I saw that his big scarred hand was trembling.

Don said quietly, 'I don't believe it. I can't and I don't.'

Victor made a sound deep in his throat, an animal sound, a growl, that came out immediately following Don's last words. He leaned forward slowly, his freckled face dead white, his green eyes gleaming. His red hair stood on end, bristling. His lips were covered with a thick white foam that dripped down to clot on his chin. He rose, growling still, and launched himself at Don, horrible, threatening sounds still coming from deep inside his chest.

Don was knocked off balance and fell over backward, sprawling. He struggled against Victor's clawing hands.

I couldn't move as the two of them smashed against my legs, then rolled away, Victor's hands still locked at Don's throat in a death grip of clawed fingers. The others, too, seemed frozen.

The terrible sounds Victor made became terrible curses, incoherent, but understandable words, poured out in a grotesque stutter. Blood flowed from Don's throat, his face. He fought back, trying to free himself. I could hardly believe that dimpled redheaded Victor, intelligent Victor, could have turned into an animal before my very eyes.

It took only seconds, but it seemed to go on for hours and hours before Dr. Paulen and Mike bent over the boys, and dragged them apart.

'Victor!' Dr. Paulen's sharp hard voice seemed to cut like a knife through the fog that must have surrounded Victor.

His hoarse stuttered curses faded away. He looked at Don's throat, then at his own hands. He stood there, held at the shoulder by Dr. Paulen, and stared at Don through horrified eyes.

'W-what happened?' he asked finally.

Dr. Paulen's smile was faint. His cheeks seemed pale above his dark beard. He said, 'I'm afraid it's all my fault. I shouldn't have let you have so much wine.'

'Wine? W-wine?' Victor asked.

'It's gone to your head, hasn't it, Victor? I guess you're not accustomed to drinking it. That, the quantity, and the heat of the fire...'

'I-I don't know. I-I was s-sitting here, and then, s-suddenly I heard y-you s-saying my name. And I was at Don...I don't understand. I don't...'

'The Group Mind,' Selena said clearly in an

absent voice.

'N-no,' Victor whispered. 'N-no, S-Selena. Don't p-put your craziness on me. Y-you're a nut, b-but I'm not. No! I'm n-not!' He looked slowly from one to another of us. When his eyes met mine, green, shining, I saw terror in them.

He stared at Don then, at the blood on Don's throat. Lastly he stared at the blood on his own hands. 'D-did I d-do that?' he asked. 'D-did I, really?'

No one answered him.

His shoulders sagged. He seemed to shrink inside his green pullover. Where there had been dimples in his cheeks there were now lines. He spread another long questioning look around the room.

Dr. Paulen said, 'Perhaps you should sleep it off, Victor. You'll be all right in the morning.'

He gave a dazed nod, went to the door.

Jimbill said, 'It's okay, Vic. Don't worry. Want me to go up with you?'

Dr. Paulen said smoothly, 'I think he'd rather be alone right now, Jimbill.'

'Y-yes,' Victor agreed. 'I'd rather be alone.' He took a deep breath. 'T-tell me the truth. Did I do that? Did I start fighting with Don?'

Again no one answered him.

At last Dr. Paulen said regretfully, 'I'm afraid that you did, Victor.'

'But-but why?'

'Just the wine, as I told you. Perhaps you

104

thought you were protecting the good of the seminar, of our concepts. That's what we had been talking about.'

'The s-seminar,' Victor repeated. He shivered suddenly. 'I-I think I-I'll go to b-bed.' He went out, closed the door behind him. It was as if he had disappeared, gone up in smoke. The thick carpet muffled his footsteps ascending the staircase.

Dr. Paulen said, 'Bess, would you play another song now?'

She swallowed hard. She held up her hands. 'Look, they're shaking. I couldn't play now. I just can't believe that Victor would...'

'But it's over,' Dr. Paulen told her. 'It's time for us to forget it. Poor Victor had too much wine and lost his head. He'll be properly ashamed tomorrow and give you a handsome apology, Don.'

'I don't want his apology,' Don answered. He got to his feet, mopping his throat with the end of his T-shirt. 'I'd much rather know what actually happened to him.'

*   *   *

The black cloud hung over me. Its stifling folds stole my breath, left me suffocating, strangling. Its stroking fingers stung my throat. Soft ugly laughter belled around me. I fought and fought, and lost, fought on, and finally I was awake. I was awake, and sitting on the edge of my bed, trembling and cold.

Some sound had saved me from the pit of terror in which I had thrashed. I couldn't remember now what I had heard over the belling of ugly laughter. I knew only that there had been a noise just beyond my door.

Selena lay still as death in her bed. I stood over her for just a moment, making sure that she breathed, before I started, barefoot and on tiptoe, across the room.

I had taken only a few steps when I stopped again. I saw at the corner of the bare fireplace a small glint of light. I went over, squatted down, peered at it. It was some kind of wire. I touched it, pulled it toward me, and it broke. I thrust it back, alarmed.

This was an old house. There were all sorts of wires all over the place. I didn't know what the one I had broken did, what it had been used for. Maybe I had managed to break an important power line or something. I got to my feet, telling myself that I'd better warn Dr. Paulen about it, and went on to the door. I stood there, waiting, listening.

The floor just outside creaked, then creaked again. That could have been what I'd heard in my dream. It couldn't have been the simple sound that had saved me. An old house was full not only of loose wires, but of night complaints and natural whispers. I told myself that I was letting my imagination run away with me. I told myself to go back to bed. But I couldn't. I was somehow sure that I had heard a sound, a footstep on the carpet. I had heard the floor creak and complain just beyond my door because someone had moved there. I touched the knob, turned it carefully, and drew the door in gently. Behind me Selena moaned, turned, then settled down again. I waited until I was sure that she was once more sound asleep, then I crept through and into the hall. It was dark, cold. I seemed to feel a wind blowing, a draft swirling around me. I could see nothing, hear nothing. I took a deep slow breath and moved toward the staircase.

From nowhere, it seemed, there was a sudden noise. Then a hand reached out from the shadows, caught my elbows.

I fought back a scream. I cowered away, whispering, 'Who is it?'

Dr. Paulen said softly, 'Jennifer, what's the meaning of this? What's wrong? Why are you wandering around at this hour?'

'I heard ... I thought ... somebody was...'

'Yes,' he said soothingly. 'That's what I thought, too, and came down to investigate. Now go back to bed and leave this entirely to me.'

'But somebody—'

He turned me, thrust me firmly toward my bedroom. 'I'll take care of it. I expected that Victor's not feeling too well just now.' He laughed softly. 'I know how to deal with that, you know. You mustn't embarrass him further by offering to hold his head for him.'

I let him lead me back to my room. I went inside, closed the door. I listened to his muffled footsteps fade away down the hall. Then the house had settled into silence again and I went back to bed.

But I didn't sleep, and when dawn came, I was up, staring, tired-eyed and frightened, at the window. It framed a steely sky from which thick white snowflakes fell in wind-driven sheets.

I dressed slowly, reluctantly.

'You'd better come down for breakfast,' I told Selena when I saw she was awake.

She shook her head, tunneling into the mattress to get away from me.

'But you have to eat,' I pleaded. 'You're getting so thin now that you look like somebody's refugee sister.'

She stared at me, her violet eyes dull.

'Selena, come on. Nobody'll be down yet. I'll make you a waffle.'

'I can't,' she said.

'You could give me a hand getting things started.'

'I can't,' she repeated.

'But you have to. I don't care if you're hungry or not. You have to come down and—'

'I can't go downstairs. No! No! Never again! I must stay right here.'

'Now, listen, get some sense into your head.'

'You won't admit it, but you know. What

happened last night do you think? You know, don't you? Why pretend with me? You *do* know.'

I thought she meant something had happened after we'd gone to bed. I thought she'd heard me moan in my sleep again. I tried to deny it all, saying, 'But nothing happened, Selena.'

She stared at me dully.

I realized then that she was referring to Victor. I said, 'Poor Victor, he must feel terrible this morning. It was really wild, wasn't it?'

'Yes,' she agreed dully. 'Wild.'

'Selena, he was just drunk. You do understand that, don't you?'

'Was he?'

'He got sick during the night, too.'

'Did he?'

'Selena...'

She lay still, pulled the blanket over her face. 'Jennifer, leave me alone. Just get out of here. Run away, run as far as you can and as fast as you can.'

I knew it was no use. I couldn't get through to her. I would have to try another time. I would have to keep trying. I made myself laugh now. I said, 'I'm going down to make breakfast. I'll bring you something after a while.'

She didn't answer me. I shrugged, went into the hall. I could hear voices from the rooms

109

across the way: Harriet and Bess talking; also Mike and Jimbill. The room that Don and Victor shared was silent.

I went down the steps slowly, wishing Selena hadn't reminded me of the night before, wishing that she hadn't brought alive all my own terrible suspicions. What had made Victor growl, spew foam at the mouth? What had made him attack Don so horribly? Had it been too much wine? Or had it been something else?

There was a rope tied around the banister. I noticed it and it reminded me of the wire in the fireplace I had broken. I hoped there was still electricity in the house. I couldn't imagine living there for more than a few hours without it.

I looked at the rope again and decided that one of the boys had been up to something. I went on down, reached the dark of the lower hallway and turned back toward the kitchen.

Something hung from the rope at the staircase. Something dangled and turned, casting a dark shadow on the floor around me. I gave it one bewildered look, and then I screamed. I screamed and screamed again, and the shadows reached out and overwhelmed me.

. . .

There were sounds, footsteps and voices. I became aware of them through swirling mists. I felt a hand on my cheek.

I heard Don whisper, 'Jennifer, Jennifer.'

I opened my eyes unwillingly. Past his

110

shoulder, I saw the dangling swaying form. I knew it was Victor. I remembered my glimpse of him, when my bewilderment had turned to comprehension, when I understood his contorted face and bulging eyes, the tongue thrust from between his lips.

Victor was dead. He had hanged himself from the stairway banister. I had been right when I looked at the rope and thought one of the boys had been up to something. I closed my eyes, sagged back into the swirling mists...

CHAPTER EIGHT

Victor's parents arrived only four hours after Dr. Paulen notified the Dean of Men. They spoke first to him, arranging to have his body taken from the Campus Health Center for burial in their hometown. Then they came to the house on Dandy Lane. They looked through the room he had shared with Don, Mr. Tarnaby and Mrs. Tarnaby, both repressing waterfalls of tears. 'He was so brilliant,' his mother said. 'He had a great future ahead of him,' his father moaned. 'We gave him everything he wanted,' his mother muttered. 'He could have talked to us,' his father told Don a dozen times.

They looked for a suicide note but found none.

Dr. Paulen gathered us together to meet them. It was a terrible feeling to sit in the living room before the fireplace, to see Bess's guitar leaning in the corner where she left it the night before, to see all the others, and to see Victor's absence as a physical thing, to remember the night before and what had happened then.

Dr. Paulen's beard looked even darker than usual against the pallor of his skin as he said, 'The Tarnabys want to know if any of you can cast any light on this ... this tragedy.'

The room was totally silent. I held my breath. I knew that the others, too, were holding their breaths. Selena sat as if in a daze, having come down when I insisted that she had to, out of respect for Victor, for his memory. I had been afraid that her absence would be noticed, remarked upon, if she didn't.

Don sat as if frozen. Mike stared abstractedly at his big scarred hands, his jaw squared and his brown forehead wrinkled. Jimbill shook his blond head from side to side. Bess closed her eyes and tightened her lips.

Harriet gasped, 'Oh, no, no! We don't know,' and jumped to her feet. She gave the Tarnabys a wild look, then fled from the room.

Victor's mother cried, 'What is it? Why won't she speak to us?'

Dr. Paulen said quickly, 'She was a special friend of Vic's, you see.' He sighed. 'It was a terrible accident. You must think of it as that. We must all think of it as that. Victor had no reason, none that we know of at least, for allowing such a thing to happen to him.' He paused. After a moment of thick silence, in which I could hear Don breathe heavily, Dr. Paulen went on, 'Unless, of course, he was in touch with you, told you...'

'He wasn't. We know nothing,' Mr. Tarnaby told Dr. Paulen, all of us.

'Or unless,' Dr. Paulen's voice was silky with insinuation, 'there was something in his background, that we, the university, would have known nothing about. An early breakdown perhaps? Or something in your family...'

'There was nothing,' Mr. Tarnaby answered.

Soon after, they left us.

*   *   *

Victor's suicide was hushed up. I doubt that more than a handful of people beyond those in the seminar knew anything about it. Somehow that made it easier to pretend it hadn't happened. At least I think that's what the others did. Nobody mentioned him. Nobody said his name. Nobody spoke of how he had attacked Don, then fled to his room.

I found that I couldn't forget him. I thought of him constantly, of the long swaying body that dangled from the banister, the bulging eyes, the protruding tongue. I thought of him as he had been the night before his death, foaming at the mouth, growling like an animal, launching himself wildly at Don. Then, in terrified disbelief, scurrying away from us to hide in his room.

It was days later, when we were supposedly deep in study again, that I suddenly remembered what had happened during that awful night. I remembered my dream, and my awakening. I remembered how Dr. Paulen had met me, told me that he had heard a sound and come to investigate. That he thought Victor was ill, and he would help him.

Had the noise we heard been Victor? If so, had Dr. Paulen gone in to help him? If he had, why hadn't he guessed Victor's mental torment? If he hadn't gone in, then why had he sent me back to bed, and left Victor alone? Or had he found Victor, found him and not aroused the house? How could he have left Victor hanging, for me, for someone else to find?

Had Victor committed suicide? Or, had he been driven to it? Why had he attacked Don, and why had he been so horrified when he found his hands at Don's throat?

I heard an echo of Selena's absent voice, saying, 'It was the Group Mind.' I resolutely ignored it. I forced myself to forget my questions.

I managed to get my midterm philosophy paper finished on time, and turned it in, not

114

satisfied with how I had done, but hoping I would pass. I wasn't shocked at the low grade I received.

I soon discovered that I wasn't the only one worried about school in the period between Thanksgiving and Christmas.

Mike told me that he was in danger of losing his athletic scholarship because his marks were so low that he might not be allowed to continue on the team.

'I don't know,' he said worriedly, his gray eyes avoiding mine. 'I keep trying, but I just don't seem to be getting anywhere, and if I lose the scholarship then I lose my chance at college. It'll wreck my folks. They've been counting on me to be the first in the family to make it.'

I noticed that Don was spending more and more time in his room. When I asked him about it, he said, 'I think I'd better burn some midnight oil. I haven't been doing as well as I should.'

Though nobody mentioned Victor, I thought he must be on everybody's mind, he, and Selena, slowly fading away before our eyes, must have unnerved us.

I determined to work harder, but concentration was difficult. I was tired, suffering sleeplessness night after night, in fear of the dreams that still pursued me.

I walked with a deep awful dread, still not quite able to identify the source of it.

Dr. Paulen seemed quite the same. The weekend after Thanksgiving and Victor's death, he built a snowman in the front yard. He decorated it with red and green Christmas lights, and informed us that he would be staying in the house on Dandy Lane through the ten-day holiday. 'Anybody who wants to,' he said, 'is more than welcome to remain here with me.'

No one spoke up then, but I saw the uncertainty cross the faces around me.

Then Harriet said, 'I've always been home for Christmas. It's my folk's favorite holiday, and we have to be together.'

We have to be together. I'll remember her saying that for the rest of my life—just as I'll remember that I saw what was happening to her, saw it, and closed my eyes to it. Saw it and refused to accept it. Saw it, and did nothing to stop it.

Harriet's quick young sexiness had completely faded away by now. She moved slowly, her shoulders slumped, her slim curved body was no more than skin and bones. Her smoky eyes were sunk deep and surrounded by dark shadow circles. Her fair skin had yellowed and even the red of her lips had faded.

She no longer spoke of her bad dreams. As a matter of fact, she spoke only when forced to, and then in a thin, barely audible voice. She had begun to look, to sound, just like Selena.

It was at breakfast time, just four days

116

before the Christmas recess. I still hadn't decided what I was going to do. I wanted to go home, to see my parents, to see Abel, too, but I somehow didn't want to leave.

The others, including Harriet, much to my amazement, had all decided to stay and announced their decisions. Each one had a different excuse, but I realized that they must feel as I do. They simply didn't want to leave. They wouldn't have been able to explain truthfully if they tried.

I was making pancakes. Harriet was supposed to be helping me, but she stood in the corner, peering away toward the gloom of the morning out of doors.

Dr. Paulen came in. He was, he said, going to try to do something with the maple syrup like what he had done once and considered particularly fine.

He took four or five spice jars and the decanter of syrup to the table, and settled there, measuring and tasting. 'By the way,' he told me, with a glance of dark eyes, 'I had a look again at the wire in your fireplace. Selena was sleeping or pretending to be, but I decided I'd better make sure that it was okay.'

I nodded. I had forgotten all about it, about telling him that I'd broken it.

He went on, 'I hope you won't fiddle with it any more, Jennifer. It works the heater in my upstairs bathroom, and these mornings are cold.'

'I'll be careful,' I promised.

He went on, mixing and tasting. Finally he said, 'Just right now, I think. Want a taste, Harriet?'

She didn't answer him.

'A taste?' he insisted.

She blinked at him, shook her head.

He offered some to me. I accepted a small drip on a spoon and licked at it. Cinnamony syrup and melted butter. I expressed my enthusiasm, but I realized that he wasn't listening.

He sat very still, his lean hands on his knees, staring at Harriet. At last he said, still not looking at me, 'Jennifer, will you be with us over the holidays?'

'I'm afraid I haven't decided for sure yet.'

'Aren't you waiting rather late to let your parents know?'

'Oh, they expect me. It wouldn't occur to them—'

'That's just what I mean. They'll be shocked if you suddenly decide not to appear. They may get worried. They may even...'

'Well, I just haven't made up my mind,' I said apologetically, knowing he was right. If I didn't turn up, my folks would be startled, worried. They might even decide to drive down to school to find out what was wrong with me. I wanted to go home. I did. I really did. But something held me back.

A strange lethargy filled me at the thought of

the seventy-mile trip. At the thought of sitting around for ten days, my parents bickering over bridge or calling the neighbors in for punch, or ... and then, there was Abel. I wanted to see him, too. But the last time we'd been together he'd treated me like a child and made me feel like a fool. Still ... he was the only one I could think of to talk to. I knew I had to talk to someone. I had to figure out what was happening. I had to. To save myself.

Dr. Paulen was saying, 'You'd better make your mind up soon, Jennifer.'

I knew what I'd do suddenly. I'd have it both ways. I grinned at him. 'I just have. I'll go home for three days, and then come right back.'

'I'll bet you your family will kick up a fuss.'

'They'll understand that I have a lot of studying to do, and that's actually true.'

'Is it?'

'Of course.' I sighed, 'I'm so far behind ... I don't know if I'll ever be able to catch up.'

'I expect you will,' Dr. Paulen assured me.

Harriet had been so still for so long that I had forgotten her presence until she said, 'You're going home for three days.' Her voice was dull, empty. 'Is that what you said, Jennifer?'

I agreed that it was, sliding a quick look at Dr. Paulen. Didn't he notice how strained she was? Didn't he see that something was so terribly wrong with her?

'We have to be together,' she whispered. 'We

always are, always have been, my folks, the kids, and me at Christmas. That's how it is.'

'Then you know what to do,' I said. 'It isn't too late to change your plans, to let them know. You can do it, Harriet.'

She gave me a blank stare. 'There must be a way.' She stood still for a moment. A look I couldn't read crossed her face. Then she said, 'Of course there is a way. Why didn't I think of it before?' She stumbled from the room. I heard her go up the steps. I heard the whisper of her boots as she went down the hall.

Dr. Paulen said, 'I wonder what she was talking about.'

'I'm scared,' I said quickly, my heart beating very fast. 'I don't know why, but I'm terribly scared for her.'

He smiled faintly. The gold emblem on his collar gleamed as brightly as his dark eyes. 'She'll be all right.' Then, rising, 'I'll ring the breakfast bell. You're all set, aren't you?'

The others soon came hurrying into the dining room, but Harriet's seat was empty.

Dr. Paulen's eyes met mine, bright, quizzical. I knew he was thinking of what she'd said earlier in the kitchen.

I got to my feet, said, 'I'll go up and see about Harriet.'

'Better leave her alone,' he told me quickly. 'She'll be down when she's ready.'

But she didn't appear for the meal, and later, when I had finished the dishes, I checked her room. She wasn't there. Bess had already gone off to class. I assumed that Harriet must have gone with her. But when Bess came to the seminar she was alone. She said that she hadn't seen Harriet. We all looked at each other across the long brown table.

'Where is she?' Bess cried. 'What could have happened to her? She came up before breakfast and said she was going out for a minute. She put on her heavy red ski jacket, tied a scarf around her hair, and went downstairs. I looked out the window and saw her at the gate, and then she disappeared into the lane. I was sure she'd be back, be here, at least, for class. So where is she?'

Dr. Paulen said, 'She's probably taking a cut again. She'll be at the house when we get back.'

But she wasn't.

We waited through that night without doing anything. We kept telling each other that she'd gone off for a little while, that we'd hear her footsteps on the porch any minute.

Only Selena said, 'No. No. We won't hear from her. She won't be back.'

Selena was right. Harriet didn't appear the next day either.

Dr. Paulen said that she had probably decided to go home. 'She was really childishly homesick, you know. Remember how much she talked of her brother and sister, of her parents? I think she was the only one of us who felt that her home was elsewhere, instead of

121

here. I expect she finally gave in to it, and went home where she could be happy again.'

I was sure that she hadn't. She had been afraid to go home, had wanted to but been afraid to. The thought of the long Christmas holiday had terrified her. I knew of her dreams. I knew of the obscene words she had heard whispered within the privacy of her mind. I knew of the horror with which they faced her. I was sure the change in her and her disappearance, had something to do with those awful dreams.

None of us ever saw Harriet again. At the end of the week, just before I was leaving to take the three days at home I was forcing myself to take, I heard the phone ring and answered it.

When someone asked for Dr. Paulen, I called him to the phone and listened as he said, 'This is Dr. Paulen. Oh! Oh, Mr. Varnum.'

I knew it was Harriet's father. I held my breath.

Dr. Paulen said, 'No, she isn't. You mean that she isn't at home?' Then, 'Oh, I see. No. No. You must understand. She left about four days ago. She didn't take her things. We all just assumed ...' He turned, looked at me questioningly. I nodded. 'Yes. It was four days, and I'm right, she didn't take anything. We naturally assumed she'd gone home and was planning to return ... No, the holiday doesn't start until today, but she was homesick, you see

... No, I don't think so. They would have told me, but hold on.' He looked at me again. 'They, Mr. Varnum, that is, wants to know if anyone here has any idea, has anyone come up with a notion since she left?'

I shook my head. He knew perfectly well that none of us knew what had happened. We had talked of nearly nothing else for the past few days. Then why was he asking me now, except perhaps to persuade them that he was really informed, really cared.

He said into the phone, 'I'm sorry. I think you'd better call the police. If you consider that wise, of course. You're sure that it hasn't happened before? She's never run off for a little while.' He paused, grimaced. 'I'm sorry. I had to ask. Well, I hope you'll keep us informed. We're very concerned, of course. So you *will* let us know, won't you?'

Eventually we were questioned by two state policemen in Dr. Paulen's presence. Harriet's room was carefully examined.

Questions were asked of students in all her classes, of her other professors. Nothing came of any of it.

Seven months later, long after it was all over, I heard that a girl named Harriet Varnum had been found after a long desperate search by her parents. She was living out west with a group of street people, begging for change on the sidewalks. She was dressed in tatters, dazed, and dirty, suffering from amnesia.

CHAPTER NINE

I could never have imagined that, though, when I left for my three days at home.

Don had said, his hazel eyes direct and questioning, 'Look, Jennifer, you *are* really coming back in three days, aren't you?'

I was startled in a way. I wondered what had made him think that I might not. What he had noticed about me that had given him the idea I might not. A soft whisper within me said, It's because too much has happened.

I made my voice firm, answering, 'Of course I'm coming back in three days.'

He stared into my eyes. 'Are you sure?'

'What's the matter with you?' I asked irritably. 'I just said so. Do you want me to take an oath, or something? Why all the cross-examination?'

'Well, you know, I've got this feeling,' he told me. He tugged at a lock of shoulder-length sandy hair and shifted his weight from foot to foot. 'I don't even know what you'd call it. Is there something like male intuition maybe?'

'There's something called male nuttiness. Of course I'm coming back. Why wouldn't I?'

Why wouldn't I? The question echoed in my mind.

I knew why. There was Selena, there was Harriet, there was Victor, and my terrible dreams, my feeling that every moment spent in the house on Dandy Lane was a dangerous moment.

Knowing all that, why did I plan on coming back? Why did I want to?

The world wouldn't come to an end if I dropped out of school. My parents would be upset, of course. They'd never understand. Abel ... he would remind me of my promise, but be relieved that I had broken it. He would think I had been so hurt by what he supposed to be my crush on Dr. Paulen that I couldn't take it any more. I could so easily escape the seminar and the fear it represented.

Why didn't I? I didn't understand it myself, but I knew that I couldn't go away for good. The strange mixture of attraction and repulsion still held me entwined in invisible webs. I could neither accept the attraction and enjoy it, nor run away and escape it. I could only wait, hoping that somehow I would be freed. Freed from what I didn't dare think. I refused to allow myself to consider it. But I know now that Selena's words were stored away in me, sucked into my psyche. *It's the Group Mind.*

Uneasily, still shifting his weight from foot to foot, Don said, 'I can think of reasons why you'd want to leave this place behind you.'

I didn't ask him what his reasons were. I didn't want to hear them. I was ashamed of my lack of candor with him, but I couldn't help it. I didn't dare talk about those hidden terrors that dogged me.

'Then I'll see you,' Don said with an uneasy shrug, finally accepting my refusal to answer.

Dr. Paulen drove me to the bus terminal. He said, 'See you in three days, Jennifer,' and gave me a long slow smile. 'I depend on you, you know. These past few weeks haven't been easy for any of us. But your clearmindedness has been invaluable to me.'

I kept remembering his smile. It warmed me through the seventy-mile trip. It warmed me so that I hungered to see it again, even as the bus drew away, and he, with a last wave, left the terminal. I daydreamed about him all the way home—and during most of the three days I was there. I found myself lonely for him with a peculiar longing. I kept thinking of his smile, his gleaming wet-coal eyes. I kept thinking of his lean tall body, and the slow graceful way he moved. Abel's warning that I mustn't allow myself to be taken by the smooth suave charm of an older man crossed my mind. I instantly repressed it. Abel, I told myself, didn't understand.

My parents pretended annoyance that I would be home only such a short time, but I could tell that they were actually relieved. They had learned to do without me, and had organized their lives to fill the vacuum I had left. Or maybe, considering it now, they sensed a change in me and worried about it and didn't understand. Anyway, my mother kept saying that I had gotten too thin, looked anemic, and that my hair was too long, too dull, too wild. My father kept asking me how school was, not listening when I made small efforts at telling him.

I was peculiarly unmoved by the beautiful tree that stood in the corner, aglitter with tinsel and blue bells and lights. The stacks of gifts, opened with forced cries of glee and gratitude, were instantly forgotten. I kept thinking of the house on Dandy Lane. I wondered what was happening there. I thought of Harriet. I slept uneasily, waiting for the black cloud that never came.

Abel came by one night. He knuckled his short dark hair, and grinned at me, and said in an irritating big-brother tone, 'Hey, Jennifer, what's new? How are things at school?'

I told him that everything was fine.

His clear blue eyes studied my face, swept me up and down. I found myself thinking of my mother's complaints about my appearance. He said only, 'Let's go for a ride.'

Oddly, though I had been hoping to see him, I was hesitant. I didn't want to be alone with him, but decent manners and memory of the past made me feel that I oughtn't to say I wouldn't. Afterward I was sorry that I had agreed.

We drove into the hills above town. He parked the car on a snowy crest and turned to me. The easy smile was gone from his face. His mouth, his eyes, were grim.

'Jennifer, tell me how things are with the seminar now. What's been happening?'

'What do you mean?'

'Remember how disturbed you were about it?' he asked.

I forced a weak laugh. 'Oh, that. Honestly, Abel, how come you suddenly take me seriously? You didn't before, you know.'

'I've done some more thinking about it.'

'Have you? And why? When you thought I was so funny and laughed your head off at me, and accused me of...'

His mouth tightened even more. 'Maybe I've been doing some more thinking about you, too, Jennifer.'

I forced a grin. 'Fine, keep it up.' A part of me meant that, but a part of me summoned all the sarcasm I could muster to say it. That was what came out in my voice.

'Stop playing the spoiled-brat bit. I want to know about the seminar.'

I twisted my hands in my lap. I remembered so clearly now that time in November when I had tried to explain my uneasiness to him, and he had laughed at me. What would he say if I told him how I felt at this moment? I could guess that his laughter would fade. A look of concern would cross his face. He would reassure me gently and immediately there would take place a few hurried and grim-faced conferences with my parents. They wouldn't know what to do, of course, so they would just get upset. My mother would cry. My father would bluster. Abel would be the one to mention emotional problems and doctors, and there I would be.

'You said something once about experiments,' Abel told me now. 'What about them, Jennifer?'

I found myself wondering about my reaction. Where did this sharp reluctance come from? Why did I so resent Abel's questions? I was terrified by what was happening in the house on Dandy Lane. Then why did I feel so unwilling to discuss it honestly with Abel— with Abel whom I had known for most of my life, had always trusted, always looked up to. Why hadn't I told him all about Selena's breakdown? Why didn't I describe Victor's suicide? Why was I concealing Harriet's disappearance from him? Something held me back. I didn't dare describe the experiments in concentration that we'd attempted. All of us at the big dark table, our heads bent, our hands clasped, Dr. Paulen's silky voice saying, 'We project ourselves from a part of ourselves, and that part is mind. We make a Group Mind that lives . . .'

I remembered the evening that Abel had had dinner with the seminar. Dr. Paulen smiling over the candle-light, saying, 'You're a newspaperman?' and parrying Abel's questions.

The conflict was more than I could bear. I felt myself being ripped apart. I clasped my chilled hands in my lap. I said, 'I'm freezing, Abel. I think I want to go home now.' But the truth was, I hadn't meant my parents' home. I meant the house on Dandy Lane.

He was silent as he drove me back to my parents' place, but saw that he kept glancing at me, giving me long thoughtful studying looks. He parked in the driveway. I reached for the door handle, prepared to slip out quickly, hoping to avoid any further talk, but he caught my wrist. 'Wait a minute, Jennifer. There's something I have to tell you.'

'It's late, Abel, and I'm cold.'

'I just hope it's not too late,' he said grimly.

'What are you talking about?'

'Who, not what,' Abel said. 'I'm talking about Dr. Paulen.'

My heart gave a quick leap, then started drumming against my ribs. I felt a chill on my arms under my heavy jacket. I was scared. I didn't want to hear what Abel was about to say.

He gave me no time to protest. He said, 'It might not mean anything at all, you understand—but it might, and I can't take a chance with you, Jennifer, so I'm going to pass on what I heard, and ask you to be cautious about repeating it.'

I looked at Abel, my lips dry, my throat

tight.

'Remember I told you that I'd heard that Dr. Paulen used to teach at a college in California and left under a cloud of some kind? I thought it had to do with his fooling around with his girl students.'

'Oh, yes,' I said sourly. 'I certainly do remember. You accused me of having a crush on him and warned me about him and—'

'Just listen,' Abel cut in. 'It just wasn't the school in California. He never settles down any place for long. He's taught in a very large number of places in a relatively short period of time.'

'And so?'

'It's a bad sign, Jennifer. You can see that for yourself, can't you?'

'No,' I said. 'No, I can't. If you're still just accusing him of being a lecher, who debauches his girl students, then I want to tell you that you couldn't be more wrong. You just couldn't—'

Again Abel cut in, 'Jennifer, look, most professors do a certain amount of changing of jobs, but they don't keep on the move year after year. I'm going to try to find out what's behind it. I'm not so sure it's girls any more, and meantime, I think you should know that there's something odd about the man.'

I thought of the house on Dandy Lane, the way the eight of us had moved into it, what had happened since. I thought of Selena, and

Victor and Harriet. I remembered the horrible dreams that plagued me. The dreams that kept visiting me there, but that had not followed me to my parents' home.

All of that passed through my mind, and then, strangely, an odd anger took hold of me. 'Why are you against Dr. Paulen?' I demanded. 'What are you trying to say about him? If it isn't the girls, as you told me before, then what?'

'I don't know exactly what I'm saying, Jennifer. I just want you to be careful.'

He knew more than I realized at that time. He had seen a change in me that I hadn't seen myself. He had put together pieces and had begun to understand. I didn't know that then.

I cried, 'Be careful of what? You're just trying to upset me, to turn me against Dr. Paulen. Why should you do that? Why should you care?'

Abel said quietly, 'The question of why I should care must be deferred to another time. Right now I just want to warn you.'

'I think,' I retorted icily, 'that you should mind your own business.'

'I think, that as neighbor and friend, you *are* my business. Also as—' he stopped himself, waited for a moment, then went on, 'you always have been, since you were a scabby-kneed little brat tagging after me to the baseball field.'

He grinned. It was plainly forced, a mere

132

movement of muscles. He patted my cheek. I knew that I was supposed to grin back, and laugh, and begin the sweet process of reminiscence that would make us both forget how close we had been to a real quarrel, a serious one.

I couldn't respond to him. My need to defend Dr. Paulen was too deep. My anger was too strong. I said, 'You should be ashamed of yourself, Abel Harding. Why, for a person like you, a responsible person, to go around spreading false rumors about Dr. Paulen is terrible. What if I were the kind of girl who'd continue that story, take it back to the campus and tell everyone about it? You could ruin Dr. Paulen. You could destroy him. And just because ... because ...' My voice faltered. Why would Abel want to destroy Dr. Paulen? I asked myself.

I thought again of the night Abel had dinner with us. He had studied Dr. Paulen carefully. He had looked at the gold-framed child's paintings on the wall. He had seemed at ease under the blue and green light of the Tiffany shade. What had happened between them that made him so suspicious now? He was more suspicious than he had been then, it seemed to me.

I had completely forgotten, by that time, that it was I who had set Abel wondering about Dr. Paulen, about the seminar, in the first place, I, in that weird uneasiness, who had actually engendered Abel's interest and curiosity.

Now Abel was saying, 'Destroy him? Why do you use words like that? I'm only suggesting that you ... that you ...'

I cut in coldly, 'Well?'

'All right,' he answered. 'I'll be blunt and you won't like it. Your behavior tonight only proves to me what I was afraid of. You really *have* developed a crush on this man. Why won't you admit it? I'm scared you'll be hurt. I don't like the little I've learned about him. He's too old for you. I can't be sure that he'll realize, and understand, what's happening. I can't be sure that he'll treat your feelings as they should be treated.'

I said sarcastically, 'As you feel they should be treated, I suppose.'

He nodded.

'Which means ignored.'

He nodded again.

I snapped the door open. I slid from the car. I stood there for a moment, gathering myself, then said coolly, 'You can't possibly know how I feel. Your suggestion is so ... so stupid that I won't even bother to answer it, I won't even bother to ...' Suddenly tears choked my throat. 'Just leave me alone,' I cried. 'Leave him alone, too,' and then I fled into the house.

I fumed the rest of the night away. How dare Abel speak to me like that? I wasn't a child. I was eighteen, a grown woman. I knew my own heart and mind. What right had he to judge me? What made him think that he could tell me who I could care for, who I did care for? I packed at dawn, and by early morning, I was on my way back to the campus. As the bus carried me over the snow-clogged highways, my inchoate anger slowly cooled, and when it did, I suddenly realized, more important, I accepted the truth of Abel's words.

From the first time I'd seen Dr. Paulen I felt some strange unspoken communication between us. I had struggled to repress my own feelings, but all along I'd been conscious of his attractiveness. I had hungered more and more for the few rare moments I'd managed alone with him, and had afterward savored them in my imagination, treasuring his smile, his dark narrowed eyes, treasuring the words of praise he offered me, the sense he gave me of being special and specially understood by him. Yet, from the beginning, too, I had felt a peculiar resistance to him, a fear that I hardly knew how to describe even in my own thoughts. Abel was right to have warned me, and I knew it. I had known it all along. I had even thought it, then refused to accept the knowledge. Then why was I going back?

Those few moments of clarity were exhausting. I closed my eyes against the brilliance of sun on the snow fields, and fell into a deep and dreamless sleep. I awakened just as the bus stopped in front of the campus terminal. I took my weekened case and got off.

The sun was still brilliant, the sky a clear hard blue. The houses on the boulevard were decorated with strings of colored lights, and each one had a tall spruce looped with glittering tinsel. I was startled to realize that it was still just a few days past Christmas. I had been gone only three days. It seemed like three weeks. It seemed like eons since I had left.

I found myself hurrying, the weekend case banging against my knees. I turned into the lane, and saw, just ahead of me, the bulky form of Mike. He was walking slowly, his brown head bent, his wide shoulders slumped, kicking through the piles of snow like a small boy unwillingly on his way home, reluctant to face the punishment stern parents would soon mete out.

Here there was no sun, only the shadows cast by the high walls of the bare bushes and the whisper of wind slipping through their tangled limbs. I tried to think of the clear hard blue sky over the boulevard, of the sharp brilliance of sunlight on the snow-covered fields. Somehow, the vision eluded me. I was faced with darkness, shadow, the drab weight of a too-long winter.

I called, 'Hey, Mike, wait up a minute,' and hurried to catch up with him.

He turned slowly. He gave me a strained grin. 'I didn't think you were really coming back.'

'You didn't? How come?'

Don had said the same thing to me before I left. I was proving how wrong he was.

He shrugged his football-player shoulders stiffly. 'I don't know, Jennifer. Don and I were talking about it. We just figured you'd ...' He let the words trail off as I fell into step with him.

'I never even thought about it,' I said, forgetting that I had. I told myself that Abel was wrong. He didn't understand. How could he when he didn't know what had happened in Dandy Lane? I felt a pang of shame, remorse. Why hadn't I told him? How I wished now that I had.

Slowly, so very slowly, Mike and I traveled the rest of the lane together. We reached the last curve, and stopped by unspoken agreement.

The house squatted behind the two tall stone pillars. Its empty windows looked down on us. I found myself shivering. My teeth chattered. A cold wind had come from nowhere to snatch my breath away and freeze my bones.

'It's weird,' Mike said softly. 'You know it? It's really a weird place.'

'Yes,' I whispered.

'It's all weird,' he went on. 'Me. I'm not a brain. Nobody ever said I was a real brain. All I can do is play football. Trying to make the grades to stay on the team is killing me, but, Jennifer, you got to admit, there's something crazy about this place, and the seminar, and maybe . . .' he added, 'maybe there's something crazy about all of us.'

I thought of Selena then. Her pale face, her dull eyes, her hopeless whispering voice. I thought of Victor, dangling from the banister, his body turning slowly. I thought of missing Harriet . . .

I managed a calm voice, repressing quick fright. I asked, 'Did something happen? I mean while I was away?'

He shook his head.

'Has anybody heard about Harriet yet? Did she ever get home?'

'No.' Mike went on, 'Jimbill's really hit, too. I didn't realize until now . . .'

'I guess none of us did,' I said quickly. 'What about Selena. Is she okay?'

'She hasn't come out of her room since you left,' Mike told me.

'Not even for meals?'

'Not for meals, nor for anything else.'

'But you shouldn't have let her—'

'Listen,' he said, his voice grave, 'what do you think I could do? Me, or the rest of us? I mean, Bess went in and talked to her. Christmas Eve we all tried, and Christmas Day, too. She just screamed at us. I tell you, it gave me the creeps the way she screamed. We told Dr. Paulen, as if we didn't know he could hear her. We said we thought maybe we'd better get in touch with her folks, with somebody. He said we better give her more

138

time. She'd cure herself, so...'

'I guess he's right,' I said quickly.

Mike looked at me sideways. 'Do you?'

I gave a firm nod, but I was thinking about Victor. There was no use in asking about Victor. It was too late for him.

Mike said, 'Don's going to be glad you're back.'

'He is?' I asked, pleased.

'He missed you, Jennifer.'

'Did he get a lot of studying done?'

'Like me,' Mike answered. 'And if I don't...'

I tried to be encouraging, 'Well, just stick to it. That's all you have to do. And if you want any help...'

'I'll holler, and I will stick to it. But you know, somehow, nothing goes into my head. I can't concentrate. I keep getting the creeps.' He laughed uncomfortably. 'Listen to me. I sound like a nervous old woman, don't I? Next thing you know I'll be looking under the beds.'

I shivered. I knew just what he meant, though I didn't say so. I'd had that feeling from the moment I moved into the house.

'Come on,' Mike said now, 'we might as well go in, I guess.'

We went up the gravel road. Here the snowman Dr. Paulen had made was decorated with glowing lights, and here, strangely, the clouds had gathered, so that even the tinsel was dull and tawdry looking.

I put my foot on the first step, and stopped.

CHAPTER TEN

'What's the matter?' Mike asked in a tone of deep concern.

I knew that he felt it, too. I knew then that each time he approached the house he experienced the same curious repulsion that I did, the same odd attraction. I knew then that even Mike, unimaginative, physical Mike, the football player, hard-headed Mike, believed in the Group Mind.

It was that sudden sharp recognition that helped me to understand myself, my own confused reactions, that helped me face them honestly at last. The barrier that I had managed to keep firm between my awful suspicions and my acceptance of them suddenly dissolved. *I, too, believed in the Group Mind.*

We had, in our seminar experiments, created this thing, whatever it was, matterless power or active potential. We had created it, and it had now set out to destroy us.

Selena and Victor and Harriet—it had taken each of them, twisted them. It would do the same to the rest of us.

This was what I had not dared to tell Abel. This was why I had turned against him in

140

frustrated rage when he questioned me about Dr. Paulen. Dr. Paulen was not the danger. It was the Group Mind.

Mike touched my arm. 'Take it easy, Jennifer.'

I drew a deep breath. I wanted to turn, to run away. I could remember Selena saying to me, 'Run as fast and as far as you can.'

I wanted to close my eyes forever on the ugly old house and will it into nothingness. I wanted to wipe the memory of the seminar from my thoughts. I wanted to forget the Group Mind—but I didn't dare.

Selena was inside, hiding away in our room upstairs. She needed me. I couldn't help Victor, I couldn't find Harriet, but I had to save Selena. I had to save the others. I could leave them to the terrible fate in store for them, but if I did, I knew a terrible fate would be in store for me, too. I would never be able to live with that guilt. I couldn't leave them. Love and loyalty forbade it, even to save myself.

With Mike beside me, I forced myself to climb the steps. He opened the door, and we went into the dim foyer together.

It was while I was taking off my jacket that I began to wonder if my real reason for staying was to save the others, or if I was concealing behind that reason another one. Was it because I couldn't face leaving Dr. Paulen?

Maybe Abel was even more right than he knew, I admitted to myself. Maybe this intense yearning I felt in that very moment, the straining of my ears for the sound of Dr. Paulen's voice, meant that I was simply entrapped in a silly schoolgirl crush. I told myself that I must accept it. A part of me felt that way. I mustn't allow it to distract me from the new knowledge I had so painfully gained. I must concentrate on the Group Mind, on evading it myself, on saving the others from it.

Mike believed in it, even if he hadn't admitted to that belief in words. I was sure of that. But what of the others? Don? Jimbill? Bess? How would they react if I were to tell them of my sudden certainty?

It was then that I heard Dr. Paulen's voice. He appeared at the end of the long hall, a dark silhouette in the usual black turtleneck sweater, black trousers, the gold emblem winking at me.

'Welcome home, Jennifer,' he said quietly. And, 'I'm very glad that you're back.'

A wave of sweet pleasure swept me. I felt myself drowning in it. I felt my cheeks burn and my eyes suddenly sting with surprising tears.

I reminded myself that I would control, repress, obliterate, that yearning part of me. I must keep my head free to deal with the problem that faced me. Suddenly I saw, and it was for the first time, that Dr. Paulen deliberately evoked that part of me. Yes, yes, I was sure of it. He chose his words, his smile. He chose his praise. I remembered what Abel had told me. Was this proof of his fears? I decided that it wasn't. Many older men engage in small but meaningless flirtations with young girls. It meant nothing at all, except that I must not allow myself to be distracted from what I must do.

I managed to say lightly, 'I'm glad to be home, too, Dr. Paulen.'

He raised his hand. 'See you later. I'm baking. I'd better see to the stove.' He disappeared and I heard the creak of the oven door.

'I'd better get to my books,' Mike said glumly. 'Though, for all the good it's doing me...'

'Where are the others, Mike?'

'Somewhere around I guess,' he said vaguely, and went slowly up the stairs.

I checked the red box for mail that might have come in my absence. There was nothing for me. I glanced at myself in the dusky mirror and saw big dark eyes filled with a new anxiety. I went up after Mike even more slowly than usual.

What would Dr. Paulen say if I told him about the Group Mind? Would he believe me? Would he laugh at me? Would he think me mad?

It was an hypothesis that we had been testing. We had been successful. Could he possibly deny that?

Why had he changed schools so often? Had he become involved with his girl students and been fired because of that? Could a mild flirtatiousness, like the one I realized now that he exerted on me, have been misunderstood? Or was it something else? I suddenly found myself wondering if he had given the seminar before, in other schools, with other students? Did he believe that what we were attempting to do could actually be done? Had it already been done? Or was it to him nothing more than an experiment, an exercise in thinking?

I tried to remember how we had embarked on the idea in the first place, moving from the study of mob psychology to the concept we had developed, but I couldn't recall the steps through which we had moved. I couldn't remember precisely what we had done, or how, yet I knew that we had accomplished something that no one I knew had done before.

I shivered, wishing that we had had failure instead of success. With failure, Selena would be safe, writing her poetry, dreaming her dreams. Victor would be studying, trying to figure out what he wanted to do with his life. Harriet would be giggling and dating, in a search for the man she would marry.

When I went into my room, I found Selena asleep on the oval rug between her bed and desk. I awakened her. I tried to talk to her. She shook her head, but she allowed me to guide her to her bed, and to cover her. Then, curled up, with her arms wrapped around her, shivering as if with cold, she went back to sleep.

I noticed that she was still wearing the clothes she had worn three days before when I went away. Soiled yellow and lavender striped bell bottoms, a soiled yellow shirt. Her hair was dull. I guessed that her lack of attention to personal things represented a symptom of her illness.

I suddenly remembered my mother's complaints about my appearance. What excuse did I have? I shuddered, decided that I must do something about myself right away.

Selena caught my attention again. She moaned softly. She was so shockingly thin. I could see the bones beneath the transluscent skin of her face. I could see a slow pulse beat in her temple.

I knew I had to do something. But I didn't know just what. I decided that I must talk to Dr. Paulen about her, and soon, very soon. But the opportunity didn't arise that day, and by the next day something else had happened.

*　　　*　　　*

Bess and I finished the salads and put them on the table. She went to ring the dinner bell, and I went to get the salt I'd forgotten. When I returned to the dining room, Dr. Paulen was sprinkling something over the salad plates.

He grinned at me. 'I sneaked a taste, I hope

you'll forgive me, and discovered you'd left out the garlic. I decided to repair the omission.'

'I did? I thought surely, when I'd made the dressing...'

'Not quite enough, Jennifer. At least not quite enough for me.'

I didn't think anything of that then, but much later on, I remembered the inconsequential moment. I remembered that, and other inconsequential moments, and I saw what I hadn't seen before.

The others came in, except for Selena. I took that as my opportunity and seized it, and when we had begun to eat, I looked at her empty chair, said, 'She's terribly sick, Dr. Paulen,' and very quickly managed to say, 'I mean, Hank. She looks terrible to me.'

'I thought you'd be able to get her to eat something,' he said, nodding gravely.

'I'll try, but she won't listen to me. I had an awful time just getting her into bed.'

'Into bed?'

'She was sleeping on the rug, all curled up, like an infant.'

He sighed deeply.

Bess peered through the auburn locks that shielded her eyes, said, 'That's how she's been for I don't know how long.'

'I think,' Dr. Paulen said, 'that perhaps I'd better notify her father. Since she isn't a student, she shouldn't be here anyway, I suppose. I thought it might help her, you see, so

146

I overlooked that, but it hasn't, as we see now. I don't think we can take the responsibility any longer.' His dark gleaming eyes moved from one to another of us questioningly.

We all nodded our agreement.

I was so relieved that for a little while I was able to forget the pressure of the gloom that surrounded me. I think the others must have felt that way, too. Jimbill told a long drawling story about his family plantation and how it was slowly falling apart, and Don matched it with a story about a trip he'd taken to New Mexico.

After dinner we all went into the living room. The small Christmas tree stood next to the fireplace, still in its finery. We set about dismantling it, putting away the ornaments, cleaning up the rug.

I found myself thinking of Selena again. I was relieved to think that Dr. Paulen would call her father but something kept troubling me. I knew she was physically sick but she had spoken about the Group Mind, and I believed her. If the Group Mind was making her sick, then how would a doctor cure her? I didn't know, but I was sure that if she were gone from here, she would be safe. I clung to that thought.

Mike hoisted the wilted tree to his shoulder and took it outside. He returned rubbing his hands together, complaining about the cold. After he paced on the rug in front of the empty fireplace for a little while, he left the room without explanation and went upstairs.

'I think he's worried,' Dr. Paulen said. 'What's on his mind? Does anyone know?'

Don answered soberly, 'If he loses that scholarship...'

Dr. Paulen shrugged, 'If he does, it would mean that he didn't deserve it in the first place.'

'Why? He got it for playing football, not for being a great student,' Don retorted, suddenly more angry than I had ever seen him, ever imagined he could be.

'Maybe being a good student is what it takes to keep up the grades,' Dr. Paulen suggested.

'That's beside the point,' Don snapped. 'They gave it to him for playing football, and that's what he does.'

'Not as well as they expected, I gather,' Dr. Paulen said gently.

Don ignored that, hazel eyes flashing, he went on, 'If he loses that scholarship, it'll break him.'

Dr. Paulen smiled faintly. 'Oh, no. I doubt that will happen. It's too hard to believe.'

'I can believe it,' Bess said. 'My grades are all slipping and I'm scared stiff, and I don't have a scholarship to worry about.'

'You, too?' Dr. Paulen asked, raising dark brows. 'What's going on here? I wouldn't have expected you to be in that kind of trouble, Bess.'

Now I saw the gentle flattery he used. It was subtle but sure. I saw Bess preen herself under

148

it for a moment.

Clear-eyed at last, I knew that he treated each of us in turn to it. He made each one of us feel special, feel important and necessary to him. It was a recognition that hurt. I had allowed myself to be deceived but I thought it to be a harmless thing. It was Dr. Paulen's way of drawing us closer to him. It was meaningless. That's what I thought then.

Bess was answering, 'I'd never have expected myself to be in such a fix either, but I have a terrible time concentrating. I just keep thinking of ...' Her voice trailed off. She jumped up. 'Let's have some music!'

She tuned the guitar, settled down on the rug. Her sweet voice soon banished the uneasiness that seemed to have touched us all briefly.

For an instant I wondered what she had been unable to say. Was she remembering how Selena was? Worrying about Harriet? Regretting Victor's death? Or was she, too, aware of the Group Mind?

As I listened to her voice, it all seemed like a distant dream. I let my mind drift. There were gentle explanations for everything that had happened.

Selena was sensitive and poetic, vulnerable and highstrung. Perhaps being too much that way had finally shaken her into instability.

Victor had been bright but repressed. The stuttering had come out soon after we all moved to the house. Maybe he had found it hard to be an outsider, hard to accept the competition of the other boys, hard to face his goallessness.

And Harriet . . . poor Harriet hadn't wanted to be in college anyway. She'd admitted she wasn't a student and giggled about it. She wanted to marry and settle down and have a family like the one she missed so much. Maybe that was why she had run away.

Yes, everything that had happened could be so easily explained, even my own wicked dreams. They might have been caused by my worry about Selena, by her proximity, by seeing her torment and hysteria.

I drifted on the sweet currents of Bess's voice. Everything would be all right, I told myself. There was nothing to fear. This was just a house. The seminar was just a course in mob psychology. I had allowed my imagination to run wild once more, creating the Group Mind to terrify myself.

I felt a glance on me, felt it with the peculiar intuition that human beings sometimes share with animals. I glanced up. My eyes met Dr. Paulen's.

Once again I had the feeling that he was able to read my mind. That he could look deep inside me and know my thoughts and feelings. He smiled faintly, approvingly, the light shining in his narrowed black eyes. I was warmed through, as if his smile was a touch, a kiss. It was a heady sensation, almost dizzying in its strength, its power. Savoring it, I closed my eyes. Dr. Paulen ... I had forgotten my insight and understanding. This particular pleasure was mine.

There was an angry shout from upstairs, a crash of falling furniture.

Bess's fingers fell away from the guitar. She raised her suddenly white face. 'What's that?'

The crash and bang were repeated. Then Mike yelled, 'No! No! Stop it!'

'Don?' Dr. Paulen asked.

'Nobody's up there,' Don said, 'except Mike and Selena.' He got to his feet quickly. He went to the door.

Mike was shouting still, but there were no words now. At least there were no words that I could understand. His gravelly voice was a raw bellow of fear and rage. It poured down from the upper room as if amplified by some gigantic sound system.

I jumped to my feet, all pleasure in Dr. Paulen forgotten. I followed Don into the hallway. The others came after me.

The crashes of falling furniture continued. Mike's bellows continued. As a group, we raced up the steps. The door to Mike's room was open. We crowded there, peering inside fearfully.

The place was a shambles. Broken furniture littered the floor. The lamps had been smashed. Books were ripped apart. The small rug had been torn up and thrown aside. The bed was broken, its springs feet away from it, its mattress spewing its filling.

Mike was perched on the sill of the open window. He was shouting, struggling. His arms flailed the air.

'No,' he screamed. 'No, no. Stop it!'

Don started in, yelling, 'Hey, Mike, what're you doing? Come down off there. Come on, man.'

I pressed forward.

Dr. Paulen stopped me, a firm hand on my shoulder. 'Easy,' he said under his breath. 'You don't want to scare him.'

Don hesitated. So did I.

Bess gasped, 'Oh, please, no ...'

With a last yell, a final struggle, Mike slowly bent backward and disappeared from sight.

We were so still, so frozen into the immobility of shock, that none of us could move. The room, the house, all the world itself, was utterly still. We heard the thud of Mike's body on the hard snow-crusted ground below. Then we heard the pulse beat of unbearable terror in the silence that followed.

I turned, ran for the steps. The others came after me. We raced down, burst outside, and hurried around to the side of the house. Mike lay still, so horribly still, sprawled on his face.

Don squatted down, bent over him. Breathing hard, he turned Mike gently.

Mike's eyes were open. His face was wet with

melted snow, with tears, with cold sweat. His tanned cheeks were tinged with green. He said, 'I must be losing my mind. I'm going crazy. I *am* crazy. I tell you, I'm crazy!' His voice was thin, bewildered, etched with the acid of fear.

'Why did you do it?' Don demanded. 'What's the matter? Nothing's worth going out the window like that. Nothing, nothing! We'd have managed something for you! We'd...'

As Mike groaned, closed his eyes, Bess ran for the house.

Soon after there were sirens, blinking red lights. The ambulance tore up the gravel road from Dandy Lane, and jerked to a stop. The attendants jumped out. They examined Mike quickly, splinted his leg and eased him onto a stretcher.

As they moved him to the ambulance, he opened his eyes again. Don and I were standing with him, close together. Mike might have been looking at Don, might have been looking at me, when he mumbled, 'You know I didn't jump on purpose, don't you? I was being pushed. I tell you, somebody was in there. He tore up the room, and then he pushed me out of the window!' Then, bitterly, 'There goes the scholarship.'

'Hysterical,' Dr. Paulen said. 'Poor Mike didn't know, couldn't possibly have known, what he was saying. After all, we were all there. We saw it with our own eyes. We know what he did.'

Bess wept, 'Oh, what's going to happen next? I can't stand it. The waiting, the awful waiting.'

'Why nothing's going to happen,' Dr. Paulen said soothingly. 'Mike will be all right, you know, a broken leg isn't such a tragedy. He'll be getting around on crutches in no time.'

None of us mentioned the scholarship, but I'm sure that we were all thinking of what Mike had repeatedly told us. Without it, he couldn't stay in school. What had happened tonight to him was a real tragedy, and we all knew it.

'I guess,' Dr. Paulen was saying, 'that he was worried about his grades. He couldn't take it and broke. It was temporary, of course; he just didn't know what he was doing.'

'You know I didn't jump on purpose,' Mike had said. 'I was being pushed. Somebody was in there. He tore up the room, and then he pushed me out of the window.'

CHAPTER ELEVEN

Two days later, Don and I went to see Mike at the campus infirmary. It was the next building down from the Health Center, and I remembered my last visit to see Dr. Barodini about Selena. I wondered what the psychiatrist would say if she saw Selena now. I wondered if Dr. Paulen had called her father yet. In the
154

excitement over Mike, I had temporarily forgotten about it.

I forgot it again when I saw Mike. He seemed, in the short time since I had last seen him, to have aged. His face had shrunken. The square jaw and ridged brows seemed smaller. His dark tan had faded. There were wrinkles that didn't belong on a twenty year old. His red-rimmed eyes refused to meet mine.

Don said, 'Hey, Mike, how're you doing?' trying for a note of cheer. 'How long will you have to be in here anyhow?'

Mike moved his scarred hands on the blanket and grunted as if in pain. 'It doesn't matter.'

'Sure it matters. What kind of talk is that?' Don asked.

'Straight talk,' Mike retorted. 'I've got no place to go when I get out.'

Don and I said at the same time, 'What are you talking about?' and stopped, and looked at each other.

I knew that Don was suddenly as frightened as I was.

Mike said, his voice harsh with anguish, 'It's my knee. It's busted. They had to take a bone out. I'll never play football again.'

A long dead silence hung over us. Then Don, obviously gathering himself, said, 'Look, there's plenty in this life besides football, and as for the scholarship—'

'Drop it,' Mike retorted. 'I get out in three

155

days. I'll go home in three days on crutches, Don. I'll live with the folks until I'm on my feet again. They won't like it, but they'll put up with it. I guess I'll ... well, I'll do what guys like me do, maybe drive a truck, or pump gas, or ...' His voice had gotten deeper and harsher, and his red-rimmed eyes got even more red.

I swallowed a lump in my throat. Mike had had such big plans, and now ...

'It's not fair,' Don said finally. 'They can't take the scholarship away from you.'

Mike answered in a barely audible whisper, 'They'd have done it anyway, Don. I wasn't doing so good on the squad. It was ... I couldn't remember the signals. I had a ...' His hands became big fists, the knuckles cross-hatched with the marks of stitches that had drawn together torn skin. 'It would have happened. It would have happened anyway, but the thing is, I don't want you to think I'm nuts. I don't want you to think I did it to myself because I didn't—no matter what anybody says, no matter what anybody thinks they saw. I didn't jump out of that window, not willingly. I was pushed.'

The evidence of my own eyes told me differently. I had seen Mike struggling, fighting, flailing the empty air with desperate arms. I had seen that no one was there. Hadn't I? But I couldn't say anything. It didn't seem the time to try to reason with him. I suppose Don thought the same, felt the same, because he, too, didn't respond to Mike.

We left soon after, and as we did, Mike said, 'Be careful, you two. I mean it. You'd better be careful because what happened to me could happen just as well to you.'

As we walked along the snowy boulevard, Don said, 'I guess Mike's flipped. It's like Dr. Paulen said.'

I heard doubt in his voice. I had the feeling that he, like me, was simply afraid to consider any other possibility. I wondered if he was thinking of Selena, Victor, and Harriet. There had been the eight of us in the seminar at the beginning. Now there were only four of us left. Four who were the same as we used to be.

Then I wondered if we four remaining really were the same. I struggled still with the bad dreams that oppressed my nights. They had returned with my return to the house. I struggled still with a nameless dread that oppressed my days, and yet, though they boiled inside me, I didn't dare openly examine, discuss, question, my ugly suspicion.

Don said insistently, 'Jennifer, what about it?'

I shook my head.

We had reached the corner of Dandy Lane. I turned into it, my steps slowing as always.

At the same time, I found myself eagerly looking ahead to seeing Dr. Paulen. I had a curious sense of hollowness, a feeling of hunger, to look into his dark eyes and watch

157

him smile. I wanted desperately to be with him then, but I shivered with a feeling of doom at the same time.

I looked ahead, and there, at the end of the lane, the squat house waited under the cloudy-heavy sky.

*   *   *

'There are always some casualties,' Dr. Paulen said.

We were at dinner that night, the four of us, trying desperately to pretend appetites we didn't feel.

Selena was upstairs, curled up again on the oval rug. She was, I supposed, another casualty, perhaps the first one. I wondered briefly if Dr. Paulen had yet called her father but I somehow didn't get to ask him then. Perhaps I didn't want to. Perhaps I was afraid to.

Dr. Paulen went on, 'We must stick together. We must be very good to each other.'

No one answered him. Jimbill played with the salad on his plate. Don chewed as if he were trying to swallow leather. Bess simply sat there with her hands folded in her lap.

I averted my eyes from them, and studied the child's drawings on the wall. A tilted tree, a three-legged bear ... child's drawings ...

Dr. Paulen's dark eyes rested on each of us in turn. 'It's sad, about Mike I mean, but maybe

158

it's for the best. He was, after all, not a real scholar, so the loss, while hard on him, is perhaps—'

'It's too hard on him,' Don put in harshly. 'If I had my way ...' He let his voice die hopelessly.

I gave him a grateful look. I didn't think I could stand to hear Dr. Paulen go on much longer. His silky voice was soothing but his words cut me like small sharp knives, inflicting pain for Mike and what had happened to him.

'We are so small a group now,' Dr. Paulen said after a brief quiet moment, 'we could, you know, easily just meet here, in the living room.'

No one answered him.

'Yes,' he said, 'that might be a very good idea.'

'It's out of the way,' Jimbill drawled, a flush on his thin cheeks. 'I mean, what about the rest of our classes?'

'Oh, I think you can all manage it without any trouble.'

'Maybe,' but Jimbill obviously still didn't like the idea. He turned to the rest of us for help, asking, 'What do you guys think?'

I didn't want the seminar to meet in the house. We were there too much already. Every hour, every moment, spent away from here, was to the good, I thought.

'It's easier if we meet at the Psychology Building the way we always have,' I said finally.

Dr. Paulen's dark eyes rested on my face. He said gently, 'Suppose we just see.'

I knew that meant he would have his way. I would never see the pale green room with the narrow window, the long dark table again. Somehow I knew in that moment, that when classes resumed the following day, the seminar would meet in the house on Dandy Lane.

*   *   *

Don's head was bent. I stood over him. The nape of his neck was smooth and white. I kept looking at it.

I clenched my fingers around the scissors handle, and felt sweat in my palms, and light gleamed on the sharp blades. My arm rose and pulled back. Then it moved in a swift descending blow...

I woke up panting. I could hear the sound of my breath whistling through my half-open lips. I could feel the pulses thundering in my temples. I clutched my aching head in my hands. The black cloud was dissolving. The dream was faint now, growing fainter with every instant.

I shuddered. The terrible things in my mind—I couldn't bear them. I couldn't! I couldn't!

Was that what Selena had felt?

Was that what Victor had told himself?

Was that what Harriet had whimpered?

Was that what Mike had thought?

I got out of bed, paced the room soundlessly on cold bare feet.

Selena groaned in her sleep and then settled down again, sucking her thumb. I had to do something for her, and soon, I told myself. Then, I have to do something for myself, too.

The sound of footsteps, stealthy on the rug and slow, but plainly audible caught my attention. I crept to the door, cracked it open. Dr. Paulen stood there. He drew me into the dark hallway. His hand was warm on my shoulder. His arm, as it went around me, holding me, was warm, too, but I shivered. Tremors swept through me from head to toe.

He asked in a soft whisper, 'What's wrong, Jennifer? Can't you sleep?'

I shook my head.

He smoothed my hair back from my brow and held me closer. Once I had hungered for this embrace. Now it frightened me. He said, 'I was checking to see if everything was okay down here.'

Did that mean that he, too, felt the terror stalking the dark halls of the house? Did that mean that he, too, was beginning to know what we had done?

He went on, asking, 'Did I wake you up? Is that it?'

I finally found my voice. 'No, Hank. Something else, a dream.'

'A dream,' he repeated. 'Ah, well, we all have

them, you know. Forget it and go back to bed.'

'Do you?' I asked. 'Do you dream, too?'

'Every night,' he answered. 'Any intelligent mind keeps working, you know. Either consciously or unconsciously. So often we don't remember what we have dreamed but the dream is there, a part of us, whether we remember it or not.'

'A part of us,' I echoed. The flash of light on the scissors ... the feel of the handle in my clutching sweaty fingers ... the smoothed skin of Don's neck. I shuddered. Why had I dreamed that? What horrible thing was part of me?

'Go back to bed,' Dr. Paulen told me.

I obeyed him. I went inside, closed the door, and climbed into bed. I fell instantly asleep.

In the morning I couldn't be sure just what was a dream, and what was reality. Had I dreamed about the scissors and Don? Had I dreamed that I had opened my door and seen Dr. Paulen standing there and told him about the dream? Had he really held me so close to him?

*   *   *

It was the end of that week. I had gone from class to class in a daze. I listened to the lectures but didn't hear them. I stared at the professors but didn't see their faces. The books under my arm were too heavy to carry. My feet dragged.

I was bone-tired, and aching. But the seminar was still ahead of me. Dr. Paulen had changed the hour that we met, and the place. Now the four of us gathered with him, in the late afternoon, in the living room of the house.

I walked slowly up the snowy gravel road, keeping my eyes down, trying not to see the empty windows. I was afraid to look. Something might be lurking there, peering out at me. Something that I couldn't see, couldn't feel, might be waiting.

I was at the steps when I first heard the sound. It was a whine of anguish and terror.

I stopped, strained to listen. I didn't want to believe it. I told myself that I had heard the wind in the huge old oaks. I assured myself that a cat was telling sad stories of being lost.

The sound came again. It took me a moment to realize that it came from somewhere around the side of the house.

I stood frozen. I didn't dare move. I didn't dare go to investigate. It was real anguish, real terror, and I couldn't pretend differently.

The whine came again, and then, instead of a whine it was a scream. I knew the voice then.

Selena!

I kicked through the snow, rounded the corner, and saw her.

She lay in a bank of piled-high snow, a tiny twisting screaming figure almost buried by blood-stained drifts. She fought the empty air, and her raw thin voice tore from her straining throat.

I saw the scratches then. New scratches on her neck, her arms. I saw them and knew what was happening.

I dropped my books, and raced to her. I bent over her, and as I did, I heard the pounding of footsteps behind me. I was suddenly thrust aside by a familiar touch.

Abel said, 'Get into the house right away. Get me a blanket. Hurry it up, Jennifer!'

'Abel!'

Where had he come from?

What was he doing here?

'Go on, Jennifer. Hurry, I tell you.'

I obeyed the urgency in his voice, the demand in his blue eyes. I raced inside, and grabbed a throw from the living room sofa.

I raced out and found Abel struggling with Selena.

'Hurry. Wrap her up. Hold her,' he said.

I managed to get the blanket around her. He folded her arms into it, his face grim, his eyes narrowed with effort. Suddenly she went limp, silent. He lifted her into his arms, held her cradled like a small hurt child.

'How long has she been like this?' he demanded.

'I don't know. I just ...' I was staring at a small jagged stone. One of its points was blood-touched. I thought of the nailfile. Had she scratched herself with that before? Had she used the small jagged stone this time? Or had something driven her to do it? Had something driven Harriet from the house? Driven Mike to throw himself from the window? Was it the Group Mind?

'Has it happened before?' Abel demanded.

'Yes, but.'

'This is the girl that had the breakdown,' he said. 'This is Selena Sellers, isn't it?'

I nodded.

'We've got to get her to a doctor, Jennifer. Right away!'

'Yes. But Dr. Paulen said—'

Abel's face was hard, cold, unfamiliar. He said, 'Never mind him. I'm taking this girl to the infirmary.'

I protested, 'Oh, you can't. Dr. Paulen—'

'Jennifer!' Abel's measured voice cut through my frantic words. 'Jennifer, listen to me. This girl is going to die if she doesn't get help. Do you understand what I'm telling you? She's going to die.'

'But he—'

Abel strode away, carrying Selena's body as if she weighed nothing.

He bundled her into his car.

'Abel, what if...'

'Stop dithering, Jennifer. I know what I'm doing even if you think I don't. Trust me for a little while is all I ask. I'll deal with him, if I have to.' Abel slid behind the wheel.

'But where did you come from? How did you happen to be—'

165

He started the motor. 'Never mind that for now. I'll explain it after I get her taken care of.'

I got into the car. I said, 'Maybe I can help.'

'That's much better.' He slid a quick smile at me. 'For a while there I was beginning to think something was wrong with you, too.'

I said, 'The campus infirmary won't take her, Abel. She's not a student.'

'They'll take her,' Abel said grimly. 'It's a matter of life and death. They'll take her, or I'll know why.'

He backed down the lane and turned into the boulevard. The lights and tinsel were gone from the spruces in front of the big houses now. The snow was knee deep at the curbs. Selena was limp, silent. I put my arms around her blanket-bound body to steady her as she tipped to one side.

'What's been happening?' Abel asked.

'I don't know. She just—'

'To you,' Abel cut in.

'Me?'

'You look ... Jennifer, forgive me, but you look terrible.'

'I do?'

'You've got circles under your eyes halfway down to your chin. I'll bet you've lost fifteen pounds. You walk like an old woman. What is it? What's been happening to you?'

'I don't know,' I said.

Could I tell him my dreams? Could I tell him my terrible suspicions about the Group Mind.

I yearned to but something held me back.

I realized now that I was trapped between two fears, between a rock and a hard place, and didn't know which way to go because there was no safe way to go.

'You told me about her a long time ago,' Abel said finally. 'You said one of the girls had had a nervous breakdown. I just didn't realize, it didn't sink in, I guess. I began to find out things, and when I saw her just now—'

'What things?' I asked. 'What are you talking about, Abel?'

'There was a suicide in the house,' he said softly. 'You didn't mention it. I just happened to pick it up. Victor Tarnaby.'

I shuddered, seeing Victor's swaying body, dangling from the banister. 'Yes,' I whispered.

'And Harriet Varnum. She disappeared. Nobody knows where she's gone, what happened.'

Tears stung my eyes. What could have happened to giggly Harriet?

'Then I heard about Mike, Mike what's his name? Justin? How he happened to fall out of a window.' He shot a clear blue look at me. 'Well, Jennifer?'

I bowed my head. I didn't answer him.

He didn't press me. He concentrated on his driving. He spun into the campus, flashed across it, and jerked to a stop at the Campus Infirmary just beyond the Health Center.

He jumped out and disappeared behind the

167

big glass doors. I don't know what he said. I don't know how he did it. But within moments, he was back. He was followed by attendants with a stretcher.

Selena was carried into the emergency room. Abel and I went with her.

When the attendants unrolled her from the throw in which Abel had wrapped her, she seemed to come alive again. She screamed, and fought wildly. The scratches glowed on her throat and arms.

I thought of the nailfile, the blood-stained stone. I didn't mention them. It took three men to hold her while quieting injections were given to her, and then it took a straight jacket to restrain her. Much later, a tall blue-eyed doctor came out to where I waited with Abel.

'It will be quite a while before I'm sure, of course,' he said. 'There'll have to be tests and examinations. We'll need a full history.' He paused, then shook his head, 'but I'm quite certain of what we'll finally find. The girl is hopelessly insane.'

Images of Selena fell through my mind, like leaves drifting down in a forest: her bright smile ... the great piles of her poetry ... her head bent under the lamp light as she read ... the dull dazed look in her eyes as she whispered, *'It's the Group Mind.'*

CHAPTER TWELVE

Insane. Selena was hopelessly insane. The words beat through my blood as Abel drove me back to the house.

The tall blue-eyed doctor had questioned me. Abel had stood by, listening, while I told what I knew of Selena's past. Her mother's desertion, her apparent dislike of her father's new wife and her notebooks of poetry. And then I found myself describing the first time I had heard her scream in pain, seen the scratches on her throat and wrists, how she had insisted that I examine her fingernails, to prove to me that she had not mutilated herself. Whispering, I spoke of the nailfile I had found later, and saw the flicker in the doctor's blue eyes. I told him about Dr. Barodini, and Selena's being sent home, and then, how she returned, worse than ever. My voice broke as I described what had happened thereafter.

I left out only one thing. I didn't dare say the words. I couldn't force myself to mention the Group Mind. I couldn't make myself quote Selena's accusations. I told myself that I mustn't repeat the product of her ravings, betray the symptoms of her madness but I know now that I must have been afraid to.

If I said that she had blamed the Group Mind, sworn that it had attacked her, then I would reveal my own belief. The doctor's blue eyes would lose their sympathy. His tall form would straighten. He would glance, questioningly, I was sure, at Abel standing behind me. He would begin to look at me as if I were Selena. So I held my tongue, and tried to pretend to myself that Selena's breakdown explained it all. Yet I knew what had happened to Victor, and to Harriet, and to Mike. I knew what was happening to me, too.

I was shocked by the sight of Selena wrapped in the straight jacket, her staring eyes, her helplessness. I was so stunned I suppose that I couldn't think coherently then.

When Abel said, 'You must have realized what was going on, Jennifer. You'd told me about her breakdown. You surely saw the changes in her,' I burst into scalding tears.

He put his big warm hand over mine. His fingers, squeezing me tight, offered me strength and consolation. I knew I didn't deserve them.

'Jennifer,' he said quietly, 'listen to me. I am not reproaching you. I am just trying to understand.'

I finally managed to choke back my tears. Weeping wouldn't help, I knew. I mopped my eyes with Abel's handkerchief. It reminded me somehow of the many times, years before, when I was in shorts and sneakers, and he was so straight and tall, helping to pick me up when I fell, drying my tears for me then, too.

Abel had been a mainstay in my life for so

long. I had taken him for granted for so long. I had been sure of him as I was sure of no one else in this world. Then why couldn't I trust him now? Why didn't I tell him the truth? What would he think if I were to explain?

When I had first mentioned my uneasiness about the seminar he had accused me of being bored, of wanting to drop the class and school. Later he had told me that I had a crush on Dr. Paulen. If I told Abel now about the Group Mind would he think of Selena's madness and look at me and wonder?

I found myself biting my lip, struggling to hold the revealing words back. The impulse to beg for help was strong, but the fear was stronger.

Abel said quietly, 'The responsibility lies with Dr. Paulen, of course.'

I gasped.

Abel went on quickly, 'He should have gotten in touch with her father as soon as she came back here. That was the first thing to have done. I'm sure Selena's family has no ideas of what's been happening.'

I found myself stiffening. 'He said he'd call them,' I told Abel defensively.

'Saying isn't doing,' Abel reminded me grimly. 'He still hasn't.'

'So many things...'

'What things?'

I shook my head.

He slowed the car, turned into Dandy Lane.

Within moments we were parked at the foot of the gravel road beside the tall granite posts. The shadowy house loomed overhead.

He said, 'Jennifer, I want to know what you are holding back from me.'

'Nothing.'

'I don't believe you.'

He took my face in his hands, turned it up, forcing my eyes to meet his. 'What is it, Jennifer?'

His touch was warm, comforting, but I shivered, pulled away.

'It has to do with Dr. Paulen, hasn't it?' he asked gently.

Dr. Paulen ... the silky voice, the gleaming wet-coal eyes, the lean figure moving with easy grace.

I said, 'Don't start that again, Abel.'

'Don't start what?'

'You know. When I saw you last you said all kinds of crazy things about him and about me.'

'Crazy, Jennifer? Or true.'

'No! Not true.' I heard the lack of conviction in my voice. 'I told you then, Abel, you and your silly ideas ... it just makes—'

'I know, it makes your blood boil,' he cut in. He smiled at me. 'You made that plain enough.' He paused. 'I was right. You're obviously allowing yourself to become more and more involved with him, and now, look at you. Look at Selena.'

'She wasn't involved with him!' I cried. 'He

had nothing to do with—'

Abel cut in once more. 'Jennifer, you were. You were, and are, so intent on him that you're not using your good sense.'

I knew that it couldn't be Dr. Paulen. It was the Group Mind.

Selena . . . Harriet . . . Victor . . . Mike . . .

I listed their names silently, and then I thought that each one of them, their very lives, had been totally changed by what had happened to them, irretrievably changed, either ended, or altered, forever.

Was something like that in store for me? Must I wait for my turn?

We had all sat at the big table in the pale green room and put our minds together. We had raised an entity, bodiless, invisible, potent. We had raised it, and now it was out of control. It would destroy me as it had destroyed the others.

I took a long shuddering breath. I wouldn't let myself consider too long, question too long. I must make the decision. I did. I said, 'Abel, I'm going to move out of the house. I think that's probably the best thing.'

He let his breath out in a long relieved sigh. 'I was hoping you'd decide that, but I wanted you to come to it yourself.'

I knew what he meant. If he tried to talk me into it, we'd have started going around the same old circle. He would be directing me, and I would resent being treated like an irresponsible child. Even if I did give in, which I might have, because moving out of the house was what I wanted to do, there was no guarantee that I wouldn't come back the moment he left the campus, while if I reached the decision on my own I was most likely to stick to it. I thought it odd how well I understood Abel's motives, how he seemed to understand mine. That was a comforting feeling, too.

'You'll move out immediately?'

I nodded. I thought then that I would. I reached for the door handle.

Abel said, 'Wait. Just a few minutes more, Jennifer. You said, just a little while ago, that other things had happened. What about them?'

Something in his voice caught my attention. There was a questioning, earnest note, a serious note. I realized that to him this was no idle question, no more than it was an idle question to me.

I hesitated for just a moment. In that moment it came to me that I could tell him. I could safely go to a certain point. I could even ask for his help, and without making him think me mad. I considered how to begin, exactly what I could safely say. I saw that he was watching me, but his eyes were shielded by dark lashes. I couldn't see into them. I couldn't read his thoughts. He was suddenly a stranger, the old Abel gone from me.

I said quickly, 'It's probably nothing but a

series of coincidences, Abel.'

He was still, waiting.

I sighed. 'And maybe it isn't really a coincidental thing at all. Maybe it happens that some kind of people, a particular kind, I mean, get interested in unusual things like the seminar, so maybe that's how come the group came together, and then...'

Abel's mouth tightened, but he said in a soft conversational tone, 'You know, Jennifer, when I'm interviewing people, asking them direct questions, I get two kinds of responses. One is quick and direct. Those people have nothing to hide. The other is evasive, full of generalities. Those people increase my curiosity.'

I knew exactly what he meant. I sighed again. 'Okay, Abel. It's just ... well, I don't quite know how to begin. There were the eight of us, you see. We met at the seminar. We got very much involved with it and with each other. We ended up living together. And then, well, you already know about most of it. First Selena, yes, she was first, but while all this was happening to her, something was happening to the rest of us, too. Like Victor, before he committed suicide, he went berserk and attacked Don, and ... and the next morning, I found him.' I stopped, choking on the memory of Victor's face.

Abel said softly, 'Easy, Jennifer, now go on.'

'Harriet, she was so anxious to go home, but

she didn't,' I whispered.

'And Mike?'

'He was so scared of losing his football scholarship. That night, when he fell out of the window, Abel, he kept saying somebody pushed him, and he said it the next day, too. Now he won't play football again because of what happened. He's had to leave school. He said somebody pushed him, and I was there. I saw it. Nobody was pushing him, Abel!' I caught my breath, stopped to stare at him. 'Why didn't you tell me you knew most of it, Abel?'

He turned the question on me. 'Why didn't you tell me, Jennifer?'

'I couldn't talk about it. It was so awful.'

'You thought I'd ask too many questions, didn't you?'

'I don't know.' But I *did* know. Abel was right. I had been afraid to face Victor's death, to think about it. Afraid of what Abel might say. Now I clenched my hands tightly in my lap. 'About Harriet, it was just before Christmas. She got very upset, and ... and ... that's when she disappeared. The police have looked for her, and her folks, have, too, of course. They still haven't found her. Abel, they might never find her.'

'Just disappeared?' Abel asked.

I nodded.

'You don't know why?'

'I thought she was homesick. I thought she'd

gone home. It was days before we realized that she hadn't. I don't have any idea ...' I let my words fade. I did have an idea. I just couldn't explain it to him. I feared that Harriet had been unable to bear her obscene dreams any longer and had fled the house to escape them. I feared she had tried to escape the Group Mind by disappearing.

'I remember her,' Abel told me. 'A pretty girl, sweet and giggly.'

I didn't answer him. I blinked back tears, and squeezed his already wet handkerchief. 'You already knew about it.'

'There were a lot of details I didn't know, Jennifer. They happen to be important details. What I did know set me thinking, but that wasn't all. I saw something changing in you, too.'

'You did?'

'Jennifer, I felt that you had to face up to it, whatever it was, to see that coincidence couldn't explain it, to be honest with yourself, and with me, too.'

'I have now,' I answered, knowing that once more he was right. 'But if coincidence doesn't explain it, then what does, Abel?'

He sat frowning, silent.

I wondered if he sensed my deception. I wondered if he was searching in the truths I had told him for what he knew I had left out. I had not mentioned the Group Mind. I had asked him to explain, but I had left out the single necessary ingredient. I was hoping that he had an answer which would negate that ingredient.

For moments longer, he sat frowning. Then he said, 'I don't know what explains it, but I'll be very glad when you're out of the house, and out of the seminar. We'll take time then to see what we can find. Meanwhile, let's not wait any more.' He touched my shoulder. 'Go on. Go inside and get your things packed. I'll move you into a hotel in town, and you can see about getting back into the dorm tomorrow.'

It was sensible. It would be much easier if I had Abel move me. But I objected, 'I can't pack up now, Abel. I want to tell Dr. Paulen first.'

I didn't realize then that I was stalling.

Abel said, 'You don't owe him any explanation, Jennifer, and now is the best time.' He paused. Then, 'That is, if you've really made up your mind to it, if you're really leveling with me.'

'I have made up my mind to it, and I am,' I said firmly.

Then I thought of Don, and Jimbill, and Bess. We were the only four left now. What would happen to them if I moved out, left them alone? What new terror would enfold them? How long before the Group Mind approached them as it now approached me?

'What is it?' Abel demanded.

I couldn't quite meet his eyes. I looked up at the house, at the gray sky beyond it. I said, 'I was just thinking of the other kids.'

He gave me a grim smile. 'You're not going to move out, are you?'

I paused. I tried to say that I would. I summoned all my strength to reassure him that as soon as I had told Dr. Paulen, I would pack and move away from Dandy Lane.

The words stuck in my throat. I knew they would be a lie. I realized now that I'd never be able to force myself to go and leave the others behind. I couldn't try to save myself and not save them. We were together in this. We mustn't be separated.

Selena had gone mad. Harriet had fled. Victor had killed himself. Mike had broken his knee. Each one had chosen a different means of escape.

I couldn't desert the few who had thus far survived, knowing that each of them, too, would eventually seek a way out of their horror.

Abel asked, 'It's Dr. Paulen, isn't it? You just don't want to leave him.'

My cheeks stung with sudden anger. 'Abel, no. Don't you see? Don't you want to understand? Why do you insist...'

He touched my lips gently. 'Stop it, Jennifer. It doesn't matter.' He leaned close to me. 'I'm not trying to play big brother now, I'm scared. I'm scared for you. I see too much. There's a pattern. It's beginning to touch you. I can't let anything happen to you, Jennifer.'

179

I didn't tell him so, but I knew there was some truth in what he had said about Dr. Paulen. I ached to think of leaving him behind, but I knew that was not what was stopping me. I swallowed hard. I said, 'Abel, listen, I'm scared, too. That's just it. I ... well, I'm afraid to move out, to drop the seminar.'

'Why?'

'Because of the others, Abel. Don, Jimbill, and Bess. They're involved, too. I can't ...'

'You mean that loyalty holds you to stay. Is that it?'

I nodded, beginning to feel better, more in control of myself. My resolve to remain had been a relief. It had cleared up one conflict at least.

'I think,' Abel said, 'that you should get them together and talk to them. I think you should explain how you see what's been going on. Tell them what you're going to do, make them see, if that's necessary, that they must do the same.'

'What could I say?'

'Just tell them that you're frightened by what's happening, that your grades are dropping, and you know that they're having the same trouble you are. Say that you think you should all drop the seminar, and move out of the house.'

'That's easier said than done, Abel.'

'It's the only way.'

'Then maybe I will,' I said doubtfully.

'Can you do it right now?' he asked. 'While I wait for you?'

I shook my head. 'That's impossible.'

'Then you won't pack now. You won't come with me now.'

'I can't, Abel. Not now, but I'll do it, I promise. I'll do it as soon as I can.'

He didn't answer me.

It was only much later that I realized that he had determined to take his own steps, but had, as he usually did, kept his own council about them. In a little while, he saw that no amount of urging would change my mind, so he left, quiet unwillingness in his face.

I watched his car bounce away down Dandy Lane, and then I went up the gravel road, and into the house. The foyer was dim and silent. I thought that nobody was in, and started up to my room. Don was standing at the top of the steps. He held a pair of scissors in his hand. The light flickered on the blade. I quickly turned my eyes away.

He said, 'Jennifer, give me a hand here, will you?'

He had a big sheet of brown paper spread out at his feet. There was a black felt-tip pen outline drawn on it. The outline of a human body, a small thin body, that reminded me somehow of Selena. It was an odd place for him to be working. I thought of that then.

He put the scissors in my hand. 'I'll hold the paper. You cut it out for me, will you?'

He knelt, spread his arms, his hands on the curling edges of the paper.

I stood over him, looking down at the smooth nape of his neck. I felt my fingers tighten around the handle. I felt the sweat in my palm. I felt the tension grow in my arm. It was my dream all over again. Only now it had become real.

Why had Don asked me to help him? Why had he put the scissors into my hand? Why had he chosen to do this job in the hallway? Why had he drawn the small figure that could almost be Selena?

Had my dream become real? Or was this a dream, too? Had I, instead of meeting Don on the steps, gone to my room? Had I fallen asleep? Was I dreaming now? Or was I awake?

A cold stillness shrouded the house. The shadows seemed to grow dark in the hallway.

I gasped, 'Don!'

He looked up at me and his hazel eyes widened. His face slowly went pale, grew smaller. He edged away on hands and knees, the sheet of brown paper crumpling beneath him.

'I didn't mean ... I almost ... Oh, my God, what's happening to me!' I cried.

I dropped the scissors, and fled to my room. I stayed there all the rest of the day, crouched on the edge of my bed, shivering, thinking of what I had so nearly done.

I remembered that I had promised Abel to

talk to the others, to ask them to leave the seminar and the house with me, but I couldn't move, I couldn't function, I couldn't plan.

I shivered on the edge of the bed and asked myself questions. What terrible compulsion had seized me? Why did I have that dream in the first place? Why had I tried to make it real? Would I really have thrust the scissors into Don's neck?

At dinner time, he tapped on the door. He called, 'Jennifer, we're waiting for you. Didn't you hear the bell?'

I had heard it, but ignored it. I didn't answer him.

He called, 'Jennifer, Jennifer, open up, or I'm coming in!'

He didn't wait for me to reply. The door flew open.

He stood there, giving me a strained grin. 'You okay?'

I nodded.

'Coming down to eat?'

I nodded again. Now that I had faced him, I knew I would have to face the others. I got to my feet.

'It's okay,' he said. 'You know that, don't you?'

'But...'

'I know, Jennifer.' He glanced over his shoulder, then came all the way into the room. He whispered, 'I understand.'

He didn't have to say any more than that. I

realized then that there were two words he was just as afraid to utter as I was, but soon, I knew, very soon now, I would have to utter them. I would have to speak them. I couldn't allow fear to stop me if I were to save the others.

Don was peering at the fireplace. He walked over to it and squatted down. His shoulder-length hair parted, revealing the nape of his neck. I looked away quickly.

Don asked in a strange voice, 'Jennifer, this wire in here. Do you know what it's for?'

'Don't touch it! It runs the heater in Dr. Paulen's bathroom upstairs. I accidentally broke it once and he had to fix it, so be careful.'

'The heater?'

'Yes, yes. Just leave it alone.'

He didn't answer me. He kept staring at the wire.

Once again the bell sounded from downstairs.

I said, 'We'd better go, Don.'

'Yes,' he agreed.

I got to my feet. As I passed the dresser, I caught a glimpse of myself in the mirror. My hair hung limp, unbrushed, dull. The circles under my eyes that Abel had mentioned looked deeper than ever. My face was gaunt, haggard. I seemed so old, so terribly old. I remembered that I had promised myself to fix up, clean up. Then why hadn't I done it?

Don was waiting for me at the door. I followed him down, carefully keeping my glance away from the back of his neck. We went into the dining room together. The candles were lit, casting dancing shadows on the walls, gleaming in the gold frames of the child's paintings. A bottle of opened wine sat before Dr. Paulen.

He glanced at me. 'After what happened here today,' he said, 'I thought we might all need a little cheering up.'

I took my chair.

Bess said, 'Jennifer, you were supposed to be helping me get dinner today. Do I always have to do everything alone?'

I mumbled, 'I'm sorry. I guess I forgot.'

Selena ... my talk with Abel ... that terrible moment with Don ... She would have understood if I could have explained it to her, but I couldn't, not then.

'And I didn't even know you were in your room,' she went on, tossing her auburn head. 'I don't think it's fair that you—'

Dr. Paulen cut in, 'This wasn't an ordinary day for Jennifer, Bess.'

She gave him a wide-eyed look. 'Just the same ...' Then, after a puzzled glance at where I shrank in my chair, at where he sat, faintly smiling, 'What's the matter?'

'Selena,' Dr. Paulen explained. He turned narrow dark eyes on me. 'I had a call from the infirmary.'

I nodded, unable to answer. It must have been the tall, blue-eyed doctor. He had said

185

that he would contact Dr. Paulen.

Jimbill drawled in a thin nervous voice, 'What about Selena?'

Dr. Paulen answered, 'Jennifer, and her . . . her friend, what was his name again, Jennifer?'

'Abel Harding,' I whispered.

'The two of them took Selena to the infirmary. She's in a straight jacket now. A straight jacket, can you imagine it? Her father will transfer her tomorrow to an institution for the permanently insane.'

'We had to do something,' I whispered. 'She was so terribly sick.'

His dark stare was steady and cold, but he said agreeably, 'Yes, of course you did. I was hoping, though, that I would have a chance to save her. I do not believe in straight jackets, you see, or in punishment of the sick. I just needed more time.'

Tears stung my eyes. Had I been wrong? Had I, in trying to help Selena, destroyed her?

'Oh, yes, of course, Abel Harding,' Dr. Paulen went on. 'The newspaperman. And how is it that he happened to be here?'

'I don't know,' I said quickly. 'I suppose he came up to see someone on campus and then stopped by to check on me for my folks.'

'I never thought it necessary to discuss it. We are, after all, quite grown up here. But I do think, Jennifer, that we oughtn't to encourage visitors, especially when the house is empty. It could give the wrong impression, you know.'

I shrank under the sting of his words, but there was nothing I could say. Once I talked to the others, it would be different. I could tell him that I was leaving. That it didn't matter if he didn't want Abel in the house, but not until then.

Dr. Paulen dropped the subject, busied himself filling our glasses with wine.

Later that evening we gathered in the living room. Dr. Paulen suggested a fire. Jimbill got it started and sat on the sofa alone. Don squatted on the floor, staring into space. Dr. Paulen took one easy chair, and I took the other.

Bess got her guitar and tuned it, and then, with a stroke of thin fingers across the strings, she opened her mouth and began to sing, but what came out was a terrible croaking noise, a gutteral howl, a sour wail that smote my ear drums with pain. She dropped the guitar. Her tear-filled eyes moved from one to another of us.

She cried, 'Oh, no, no! Now it's after me!'

CHAPTER THIRTEEN

We all sat in frozen silence. No one answered her. No one spoke. The flames cracked in the fireplace and the wind sighed at the window. After a moment, she got up, and staggered from the room.

Dr. Paulen smiled faintly, then said, his voice dry and amused, 'I think Bess has overestimated her ability to drink wine.'

Again no one answered, no one spoke.

I looked from face to face. I studied Don, then Jimbill. Finally I studied Dr. Paulen himself. The gold emblem glittered on the roll of his turtleneck sweater, and there were points of gold in his wet-coal eyes.

There had been something faintly familiar about what he had just said. The wine ... the wine.

Then I remembered. Victor, he had told us, had had too much wine and been sick in the night. In the morning Victor had been dead.

I looked back at Don, at Jimbill. I saw knowledge and recognition there. I saw understanding. They knew what Bess had meant. They knew who was next. They also believed in the power of the Group Mind.

The dark cloud came swiftly and suddenly. It hung over me, stifling my breath. It stroked fire along my arms and throat. From within it, whispered chuckling laughter, and when finally the laughter faded and there were words—terrible words, obscene and frightening, poured over me.

A face took form in the cloud. A lean face with gleaming black eyes, with a carefully trimmed mustache and a black beard. It smiled. Its lips moved. It was the face of the Devil, the face of the Group Mind. It was Dr.

Paulen! He was leaning over me, speaking softly...

*　　　*　　　*

I awakened at dawn, clammy with cold. Snowflakes whispered against the window pane. I sat up slowly, shuddering. Had I been dreaming? Or had Dr. Paulen really stood over me, whispering? A strange urgency possessed me. I had to go out into the air, into the snow.

Something glittered on the oval rag rug. I stared at it for a long time before I went over, picked it up, turned it in my fingers. For a moment, I didn't realize what it was, then I recognized it. It was the gold emblem that Dr. Paulen always wore.

What was it doing here? How had it come to be in my room? When had he dropped it or put it there? I didn't know the answers to those questions. I found it hard to concentrate. The urgency within me to go out of doors was growing stronger.

I started from my room, holding the gold pin. The hallway was dim in the dawn. I was at the head of the steps when Don's door creaked open.

He looked out, frowned, whispered, 'Jennifer, wait a minute.'

'I can't. I have to—'

'What's that?' he demanded in a suddenly harsh whisper. 'What's that thing you're holding?'

My feet moved impatiently, turning me toward the steps.

He grabbed my shoulder, jerked me into his room, and closed the door.

I said, 'Look, Don, I don't know what's bothering you, but I just have to—'

'Be quiet.' He took the pin from my fingers, the pin I had already forgotten. He stared at it. 'Where did you get this, Jennifer?'

'It was in my room. I just—'

I stopped, stared at him. I was remembering the dream now. Dr. Paulen . . . bending over me . . . whispering . . .

But it hadn't been a dream. It had been real, or at least a part of it had been real. He had been in my room. He had dropped the small gold emblem then.

Don said, 'You can't go outside, Jennifer.'

'Why not?'

He said, as if to himself, 'Maybe it was the wine.' Then, 'Jimbill's sleeping as if he's drugged, so is Bess.'

'How do you know?'

'I went into their rooms and checked.'

'Then why aren't you . . .'

He smiled faintly. 'I didn't drink it.'

'But I did.'

'Yes,' he said thoughtfully. 'You did, didn't you?' Then, putting the pin in his shirt pocket, 'Don't mention finding this in your room, Jennifer. Let me keep it. When I give it back to

Dr. Paulen, I'll tell him I picked it up on the stairs.'

We looked at each other for a long moment. Then I felt the pressure of the urgency again. I whispered, 'I'm sorry, Don. I have to go outside. I just have to.'

He took my hand. 'All right. We'll go together.'

We walked through the falling snowflakes, hand in hand. We didn't try to talk. The heavy brooding silence was broken only by the whisper of the wind. The dawn brightened and then slowly grayed again. At last the urgency slackened, was gone. My legs would hardly hold me. I said, 'We'd better go in, Don.'

He said, 'Jennifer, no matter what happens, don't go outside by yourself. You understand me? Don't leave the house alone.'

I nodded, but I was thinking more about Dr. Paulen, how he had leaned over my bed, the gold emblem on the oval rug. I was thinking about the compelling urgency that had aroused me, driven me outside.

Don had said he thought that Bess and Jimbill were drugged because they were sleeping so soundly, while he, who had not drunk the wine, was wakeful. But what about me? I had emptied my glass. Then I realized that I had slept heavily, dreamed terribly, but I had been awakened. The wine . . . Dr. Paulen's voice . . . the compulsion that had driven me . . .

Don insisted, 'Jennifer, do you hear me? Will

you call me if you ever feel that way again?'

I nodded.

He said nervously, 'What's the matter? Can't you talk?'

'Yes, I can, but...'

'You're staring at me, Jennifer. Your eyes look funny, the pupils so big, I just realized. Maybe it's the wine. But you look—as if you've been hypnotized.' He stepped back from me. 'Go on inside.'

'Hypnotized?' I whispered. 'Don? Is that what you said? Hypnotized?'

Now he stared at me. There was fear in his hazel eyes. His lips moved, but I didn't hear what he said.

Past his shoulder a light flashed on in the kitchen window. Dr. Paulen stood there, looking out at us.

*   *   *

Abel had said that Dr. Paulen's name was familiar. Later he told me that Dr. Paulen had taught at a university in California and left there under a cloud of some kind, having to do with his relationship with his girl students. Some time after that Abel had said that Dr. Paulen had transferred from one college to another, staying in each place only one year. I considered that and wondered what it added up to. I saw no way in which it could explain what was happening in the house on Dandy

192

Lane.

Don had mentioned the possibility that the wine had been drugged. When he said that I acted as if I had been hypnotized, I realized suddenly, that I might actually have been. Dr. Paulen had been at my bed, talking to me while I slept, while I dreamed of the amorphous black cloud. I was sure he had been there. The gold emblem proved it to me.

I struggled to deal with my chaotic thoughts. If I put aside the Group Mind, if I thought only of concrete reality, could I explain everything that had happened? I didn't know, but I could try.

Right after my philosophy class, in which I had heard not a single word, I went to the library. I found the collection of biographies of the various professors at the school. Dr. Paulen's was brief indeed, composed only of four lines. It told where he had studied, listed three schools at which he had taught. It told nothing else about him.

I didn't know what step to take next. I considered for a long time. Then I called Abel. Abel was experienced, sensible, trustworthy. He already knew so much of what had happened. He would be the one to help me, I was sure. Why had I doubted him before?

I couldn't reach him at home or at his office. I tried over and over, but still couldn't get through to him. I sat in the library, trying to think what I could do. The afternoon passed.

The snow stopped. It was time for me to go back to the house. I didn't want to, but I could feel the hunger begin to grow in me.

Finally, I gathered my things, put on my jacket. I went trudging down the boulevard. A horn blew at me. I turned my head away. A car pulled up, heading in the other direction. Abel leaned out and yelled my name.

I ran to him, half weeping, half laughing. I fell into the car. 'I didn't know it was you at first. Oh, Abel, how did you find out I needed you? I've been phoning you for hours and hours. I never thought I'd see you now ... I just...'

'I've been hours looking for you,' he told me. 'I just checked the house again, and you still weren't there.'

'I was at the library.'

'Why did you phone? What's happened?'

I heard the raw anxiety in his voice and I said quickly, 'I'm all right, Abel, but I had to talk to you.'

'That's why I'm here.' He put his hand on mine. 'I've done some digging, Jennifer. What I've got to tell you—' He stopped, looked at me sadly. 'Just remember that I'm not trying to harm Dr. Paulen. I'm trying to help you, and the other kids in the house.'

'I've done some digging, too,' I said quietly. 'I looked Dr. Paulen up in the biographies. There was nothing there.'

'I know. I went over them first.' Abel looked

startled, then pleased. 'What made you go to them, Jennifer?'

Quickly I told him about the night before. I told him about finding the gold emblem on the oval rug after what I was sure now had not been altogether a dream. I told him about Don's suspicion of the wine. I described how Don and I had walked through the dawn hours, he accompanying me while I suffered through a compulsion I couldn't control, and how Don had said I looked hypnotized.

At last, slowing down, breathing hard from having talked so long and quickly, the information I had given him added up in my own thoughts. It was organized now. It formed a pattern. Abel, too, had thought he'd seen a pattern. He'd said so just the day before. I said, 'Abel, there's no Group Mind, is there? There couldn't be, could there?'

His face was grim. 'I don't know if there could be, Jennifer, but there isn't, not here, not now. It's Dr. Paulen's mind.'

I thought of Selena. Had she been hypnotized, drugged? Had she been driven to tear her flesh with the nailfile? Selena, the vulnerable one, first of all of us to fall under the spell? Then Victor, hypnotized, or drugged, into attacking Don? Had he been driven to suicide by the thought of what was happening to him? Harriet ... Mike ... I thought of those four destroyed ones and felt sick.

'But why?' I whispered. 'Why, Abel? If he's

195

responsible, if he was just using the seminar to drive us all mad, then he had to have a reason.'

I moved close to Abel, seeking warmth and comfort and safety from him. He put an arm around me. I went on, 'It can't be for nothing, Abel. No one could be that cruel for nothing.'

Abel reached into his pocket, drew out some photostats. 'It was easy, once I really started looking. The only thing was ... it took time, and I didn't know for sure how much time we had.'

He held the clippings out. My hand shook as I accepted them. I read them slowly, trying to absorb their importance. The first was a big write-up about a thirteen-year-old child prodigy named John Paulen, the only son of Dr. Henry Paulen and Mrs. Mary Paulen. The boy had been accepted at a university in the Southwest. I thought of the gold-framed child's drawings on the walls of the dining room: a tilted tree, a house, a bear.

The second clipping was about the death of John Paulen, age fifteen, honor student, at the same university in the Southwest. It said that John, injured during a fraternity initiating ceremony, had died on the way to the hospital. I shuddered. Tears stung my eyes.

The third said that the death of Mrs. Mary Paulen, wife of Dr. Henry Paulen, and mother of John Paulen, who had recently died in a fraternity initiation, had been declared a suicide.

The boy John, the wife Mary, had died. But Dr. Paulen lived on, remembering, hating. I knew what had driven him. I knew it had driven him mad. He must be mad. There could be no other explanation. His hatred for students was a mad hatred, even if I could sympathize with his pain, pity his agony.

I thought of Selena and Victor and Harriet and Mike. I thought of the terror on Bess's face, and the grimness in Don's, and Jimbill's growing watchfulness. I thought of my own anguish.

I put the clippings into Abel's hand, glad to relinquish them. I said, 'I'm sorry for him, Abel. What should we do?'

'We have to get the rest of the kids out of there first. Then we'll go to the administration. I'll show them these clippings. We'll tell them everything that's happened. The rest will be up to them.'

'The rest?'

'Jennifer, the man is—' Abel stopped himself. 'You know the answer to that.'

'He's mad,' I said quietly.

Abel nodded. 'But we have no proof. You do realize that?'

'We'll have to find proof,' I said. 'Maybe the wine, maybe other things.'

Abel nodded. 'If we can, but more importantly, we'll have to get the kids out of there.'

'*I* have to,' I said. He looked as if he might

197

argue. I said quickly, 'Abel, if you come into the house Dr. Paulen will . . . well, I don't know what he'll do, but I think it's better if you don't.' I didn't wait for an answer. I looked at the lowering sky. 'It's getting late. We'd better go back to the house right now.'

Abel started the car, made a wide U-turn, and drove out to the boulevard. He slowed at Dandy Lane and turned in. Within moments, we were parked before the house.

I looked up at the empty staring windows. 'I don't know if he's there.'

'If he is, just act as naturally as you can, but be careful, Jennifer. You mustn't let him suspect anything. At the first opportunity, get the others together. Talk to them. Tell them everything we know. Get them out of there tonight.'

I nodded.

'Remember I'll be close by. I'll be watching every minute. If something happens and you can't convince the others, or you find that you can't get out, then throw a handkerchief from a window, or light a match in front of one. I'll be touring the house all the time. I'll be watching for you.'

*   *   *

We were in my room. Bess sat beside me on the bed. Don and Jimbill sat on the floor.

They passed the clippings from hand to

198

hand. When they had all read them, they sat quietly staring at me.

It was nearly midnight, but I hadn't been able to talk to them before. Dr. Paulen had been in the house when I left Abel.

He said, 'I see your boyfriend is back again. I'm surprised at you, Jennifer. After what I suggested.'

'My friend, not boyfriend,' I protested, my cheeks burning, my eyes avoiding his.

'Whatever he is.' Then, 'I thought we'd agreed that he wouldn't be hanging around here anymore, Jennifer.'

'I ran into him on campus and he drove me back,' I said as coolly as I could, and escaped by going into the kitchen.

It was while I was cooking that I suddenly remembered how often he came in, watched while I, the others, worked. How often he tasted, added things, or carried in the coffee pot. Now I understand his interest in the kitchen. It must be that one of the opportunities he used was the kitchen visit. Then he could easily have put something into the food we ate, the coffee we drank. It needn't have been just the wine. We could have been given sedatives, hallucinating drugs, and even poisons. Selena's delusions, Victor's wild behavior, Mike's fight with the empty air, Harriet's despair —each one of them showed symptoms compatible with mind-altering drugs. I shuddered as I worked, relieved that he hadn't followed me, that he wasn't there then, watching me.

There was no wine at dinner. I tasted the food gingerly, but could identify no foreign substances. I decided that perhaps that night, for some reason of his own, he had not doctored anything.

Don had given him the gold emblem, saying, 'Oh, Hank, I almost forgot. I found this on the steps this morning.'

Dr. Paulen thanked him, said, 'It once belonged to my son,' and his gleaming dark eyes went to the child's drawings on the wall. When dinner was finished he withdrew to his third floor study, to work, he said.

The rest of us went to our rooms. I waited for hours before I gathered them together. Now, facing the bewildered faces before me, I tried to think where to start.

Don suddenly pushed himself to his feet. 'Wait a minute, Jennifer. I just thought of something.' Then, 'Hey, Jimbill, come look at this, will you?'

He led Jimbill to the fireplace, pointed out the wire. 'That's for the heater in the bathroom upstairs.'

Jimbill retorted. 'That's not what it is.' He bent closer, then grunted. 'Oh, yeah, I see where it goes.' He traced the wire to under my bed and grunted again. 'What do you know? A bug. Now who'd bug Jennifer's room?' He wrapped his hand in the wire, jerked twice, and the whole thing came free in his hand. He tossed it aside, came back to sit before the bed. Don joined him. 'Okay. Now we know about the bug, and we know about Dr. Paulen's past. What has it to do with us?'

'Or with the seminar?' Jimbill drawled.

'Or with the Group Mind,' Bess whispered.

CHAPTER FOURTEEN

If I had had any wavering doubts before, they were completely gone now.

I didn't know what use the bug had been put to, but I knew that only Dr. Paulen could have installed it. I had a sudden sharp picture in my mind of him sitting in his third floor study, amid the tangle of wires I had noticed there, listening to my conversations with Selena, hearing her screams. That image lent urgency to my voice. I said, 'There is no Group Mind.' I leaned forward, looking from one to another of them. 'Don't you understand me? There is no Group Mind at all. It's Dr. Paulen. He's the mind, the only one that's been doing all these things to us, things that finally drove Selena insane, and Harriet to disappearing, and Mike to breaking his knee, and Victor to killing himself.'

Jimbill drew his breath in sharply.

Don nodded, his eyes on the ripped-free

wires.

Bess shook her auburn head from side to side. 'I know. I know how I feel, what things are in my head. I'm glad we can talk about it now. I never dared to before. But you can't say it's Dr. Paulen, it isn't. It's the Group Mind that we made in the seminar. We're all responsible for it, not just him.'

'Where did you get these clippings?' Don asked, ignoring Bess as if she hadn't spoken.

'Abel checked up. He got them and brought them to me.'

'Where's Abel now?'

'He hid the car, I think. He's out there, though, waiting for us to come out. We arranged to drop a handkerchief out of a window, or light a match, in case we run into trouble.'

Jimbill asked, 'How do you know he didn't fake it? Or that the Group Mind didn't plant the information?'

'You're wasting time,' I cried. 'We've got to get away, while we can.'

Jimbill considered, then drawled, 'But if we're wrong, and we turn the Group Mind against us, anything can happen. I'm afraid to take that chance.'

Bess nodded vehement agreement.

'The bug, Jimbill,' Don said. 'That's something a *man* put in.'

Bess and Jimbill shook their heads.

Don said, 'Let them stay if they want. The

202

two of us can get out, get help.'

'I can't leave them here,' I cried. 'I can't do it, Don.'

Bess muttered, 'I'm afraid to go out into the dark.'

'We don't know what will happen if we do,' Jimbill agreed.

I waited for a moment, gathering myself, thinking of the best way to convince them. Finally, I said, 'You remember how it started in the seminar, don't you? We were talking about mob psychology, and then we got on to the idea of a new and individual consciousness that couldn't be controlled.'

They nodded.

I went on. I told them that I thought Dr. Paulen, with a few words here and there, directed our imaginations, led us to that concept. He slowly and carefully built up to it, so we could accept it. Then, once we had all moved into the house, the idea already firmly implanted in our minds, he began to make it seem that we had been successful. I reminded them of how often he was in the kitchen, how easy it would have been for him to administer all kinds of drugs to us, in our food, in our wine. One after another, things happened. Four of us went down. But we were all affected. 'Look at us. We're lethargic. We don't take care of ourselves. We've all lost a lot of weight. Those are drug symptoms. There's that bug that Jimbill ripped out. I'll bet if we search the other rooms, we'll find more of them.' I took a deep breath. 'And I'm pretty sure, thinking about it now, that he did other things, too. A couple of times I've found him down here, on this floor, in the middle of the night. Once I dreamed he'd been talking to me while I slept, and I found his gold pin on the rug the next morning.' I looked at Don for confirmation, and he nodded. 'I think Dr. Paulen was here, speaking to me, planting post-hypnotic suggestions that I'd follow afterward. I've had the feeling so many times that I was driven to do something, that I just had to, even if it didn't make sense.'

Don nodded again. 'Yes. I've had that, too.'

Then Bess said, 'But it's the Group Mind, not Dr. Paulen.'

I hesitated, not knowing how I could make her, make Jimbill, see the danger, and then, quite suddenly, I knew the right words. I said quietly, 'All right. Maybe you two have the answer and I'm wrong about this. Suppose there is a Group Mind. If we know anything about it, we know it's evil. We know it's going to destroy us all. We have to stop it. We have to get away. Don't you see that you're only holding back because that's what it's telling you to do? That's what it wants? Never mind Dr. Paulen, or the clippings, or even the eavesdropping bug. Just think of one thing. The Group Mind wants you to stay here so that it can do to you what it did to Selena and Victor

204

and Harriet and Mike.'

Exhausted, breathless, I stopped.

There was a brief silence.

Then Jimbill rose, sighing. 'I guess that's right,' he said quietly. 'We'd better get out of here.'

Bess rose reluctantly, 'If you're all going, then I'd better go, too.'

But I could see that she wasn't quite convinced it was the best thing to do. She was simply scared to be making any move. She hung back as we left the room together. She kept peering over her shoulder as we crept down the steps. We got as far as the foyer. Holding my breath, I tiptoed toward the door. I eased it open.

That was when a great echoing explosion shook the house. Light flashed and faded into dark. Plaster crumbled. Glass shattered in flying shards. Blinded, deafened, I stumbled and fell.

Abel appeared in the shadows. He caught me as I went down, dragged me to my feet, thrust me outside, and ducked through the door again.

Great clouds of steamy bitter-smelling smoke poured out, and the red glow of flames began to grow larger.

Bess staggered out, weeping, clinging to Jimbill. Abel finally returned, pulling Don with him. We crept off the burning porch, and from the yard, we stared up at the house. All its windows were alight with leaping flame now. Steam and smoke rose from them in loose billowy clouds. Abel hugged me briefly, then raced away to sound the fire alarm.

He was back within moments and holding me again when Dr. Paulen appeared at a lower window.

He stared out, his dark head wreathed with smoke. He laughed, and it was like in my dream. Soft, chuckling, horrible laughter. He yelled, 'You created a monster and it will pursue you for the rest of your days. You are marked, and it will follow. The Group Mind will destroy you!'

Then around him there were flames. His whole dark-clad body was aglow with them, alight with the hungry lips of the fire.

'You'll die as my son died,' he screamed, and then suddenly, the flames leaped higher, blinding me, just as his words choked my heart. When I could see again, breathe again, he was gone.

'It's over,' Abel said quietly.

I shivered. Was it really over? Moments before, trying to persuade Bess and Jimbill, I had been so sure, but now I wondered. Were Abel and I right? Did Dr. Paulen plot to destroy those in the seminar? Or had we somehow raised a strange entity with a will of its own, a disembodied mind that set out to kill us one by one? To kill us, or to drive us to madness and then to suicide.

Red lights blinked on the lane, and sirens shrilled. Fire trucks rolled up the gravel road past the gray stone pillars, but they were too late. The house on Dandy Lane was doomed.

*   *   *

The papers described it as a tragic accident. Only a few of us knew differently.

The firemen found evidence of a bomb explosion, and privately listed the fire as arson, and Dr. Paulen's death as suicide.

They found vast quantities of wires running from Dr. Paulen's third floor study to each of the second floor rooms. They were puzzled by them, but Abel was sure that they were the remains of eavesdropping devices that Dr. Paulen had used, and that, listening through them before Jimbill had detached the one in my room, Dr. Paulen had realized that the story of the tragedy of his past was known and that we would soon leave him. That was why he had blown up the house.

I left Dandy Lane without looking back, without even wanting to look back. I felt free for the first time in months.

Bess and I moved into the dormitory the next day.

Abel went back to his job.

A few days later Don called, asked me to meet him. We had lunch together.

He said, 'Jennifer, I have to get away from

here. I can see it's no good. I think about what happened all the time.'

'Give yourself a chance,' I said. 'It'll get easier. I'm sure that it will.'

'No.' He smiled wryly, tugged at his shoulder-length hair. 'I already know it won't. I'm going to quit, get myself a job.'

I thought that Dr. Paulen, the Group Mind, had managed to alter Don's life, too. He should have gone to school, law school. He should have been a lawyer like his father.

Don went on, 'What I want is ... well, listen, Jennifer, come with me, be with me. We'll get married. We've been through so much together, and seen so much, I think we must belong to each other now.'

I shook my head slowly, regretfully. I said in as gentle a voice as I could summon, 'Don, I'm sorry. I can't do that.'

'But why?' he begged. 'Why should we both be alone?'

'I can't,' I repeated.

I didn't want to tell him my reason.

I was waiting for Abel. He was gone now, but I knew he'd be coming back. He'd be coming back for me soon.